MADRIGAL FOR CHARLIE MUFFIN

Charlie dried his face and was reentering the bedroom when the telephone which never rang jarred through the tiny apartment. His immediate reaction was one of fear. He watched it for several moments and then reached out hesitantly.

'Hello?' There was still a vague fog of alcohol in his voice.

'Charlie,' said the voice. 'I've been calling you for hours. It's Rupert Willoughby.'

Charlie had rehearsed the approach but when the time came he couldn't think of the prepared words. Instead, he said, 'I'd like to see you.'

'Good idea,' said the underwriter. 'I've got a bit of a problem.'

It was a measure of how careless Charlie had become that he talked unaware of the listening device that had been implanted in his receiver. In the early days he had dismantled it regularly, but, as with everything else, he hadn't bothered for months.

Also in Arrow by Brian Freemantle

MADRIGAL FOR CHARLIE MUFFIN

Brian Freemantle

ARROW BOOKS

Arrow Books Limited
62–65 Chandos Place, London WC2N 4NW

An imprint of Century Hutchinson Limited

London Melbourne Sydney Auckland
Johannesburg and agencies throughout
the world

First published in Great Britain by
Hutchinson 1981
Arrow edition 1982
Reprinted 1987

Printed and bound in Great Britain by
Anchor Brendon Limited, Tiptree, Essex

ISBN 0 09 930020 6

For David and Patricia, hoteliers
extraordinary! With much love

I am always with myself and it is
I who am my tormentor

Tolstoy *Memoirs of a Madman*

Prologue

It was an assassination method the Russians had perfected, the bullet soft-nosed and lightly packed, from an adapted Tokarev automatic. There had been no exit wound, just an instantaneous explosion of the heart. The photograph showed no distortion of the features: the dead man looked as if he might awaken at any moment, just like the others had done. Sir Alistair Wilson was surprised at that. He would have expected an expression of pain. The intelligence director pushed the latest file away, knowing there was nothing he could learn from it. Delhi, Ankara and now Bangkok: and he was no closer to the traitor now than he had been six months ago, when the killings of embassy intelligence Residents started.

Wilson felt impotent, having to rely so completely upon Alexander Hotovy. The man's defection from the Czech embassy in London had been agreed when the assassinations began. And was immediately postponed, for Hotovy, a major in the Statni Tajna Bezpecnost, the Czech intelligence service, to earn his asylum by discovering how the British operatives were being pinpointed. The initial response had been encouraging: perhaps too much so. Within a week, Hotovy confirmed that all Eastern bloc embassies were receiving, via Moscow, details of British cabinet guidance to overseas ambassadors, together with personnel details from which it was easy to isolate intelligence officers in the field. Then came the stalemate. By the time the guidance arrived from Russia, all indication of original source had been removed. Which meant Wilson knew he had a spy in a British embassy somewhere in the world, but not which one. The trap had seemed feasible, even clever, when he devised it. That had been six months before and since then two more people had died.

The irritation of his own ineffectiveness was showing on Wilson's face when he looked up at his deputy's entry.

'It's worked!' declared Peter Harkness.

For a moment Wilson didn't speak. Then he said: 'Sure?'

'Positive.'

'Thank God for that!' How long would it take, he wondered.

General Valery Kalenin's car was an official Zil, authorized to use the exclusive centre lane of Moscow roads, but the traffic at night was light, so the privilege reserved for members of the Soviet hierarchy was unnecessary. Kalenin's driver still used it; he enjoyed the advantage of power more than the KGB chief. The Zil swept past Kutuzovsky Prospect and the Kremlin towards Dzerzhinsky Square. That day's overseas files and reports were waiting for him, neatly arranged in order of their late-afternoon transmission. Kalenin unfastened his jacket, lit a tube-filtered cigarette and settled down to work. He read steadily and carefully, annotating margin notes from which his deputies could initiate action the following day.

For years Kalenin had maintained an office cleaner at the British embassy in Cairo. Usually the information was of low-level interest, little more than the occasional indiscretion from a waste-paper basket, from which they had to make a surmise. But sometimes there was something worthwhile. Like tonight. Kalenin had a retentive memory and saw the significance at once. A meticulously cautious man, he went to the filing cabinet where the intelligence from his top agents was kept and located at once what he wanted, turning the shade of his angled light upon an identical message he had received a month earlier. Identical but for one thing. The source of the first message was listed as Cape Town. The origin of the second, which he had upon his desk, was given as Lagos. From the advice docket attached to the initial information he saw that it had been transmitted a week before to the Warsaw Pact capitals, for guidance to their embassies.

Kalenin returned to his desk and for a long time stared sightlessly at the wall. A trap had been set and he had fallen into it: and it could hardly have happened at a worse time. The qualification came almost at once. If he were clever, it could be worse for others.

British and Soviet intelligence operations began within twenty-four hours of each other, one to uncover, the other to conceal.

The Russians had the advantage. Kalenin had anticipated the possibility and had the framework of a protection operation ready. He went again to the filing cabinets, for the dossier on Charlie Muffin.

1

Charlie Muffin jarred stiff-kneed along Cheyne Walk, head
bent to concentrate upon the pavement cracks. Easy to make
a straight line; always had been. Just fix on the pavement
joins and left right, foot either side, like the police-station
tests in the old days, before the breathalyzer. Done it a dozen
times pissed as a monkey. Never pulled department weight,
until it became absolutely necessary. Rarely had been.
Always able to make the straight walk, enunciate the trick
phrases from the card, without denting the words. Sherry's a
difficult one, when you're Brahms and Liszt. Always clever
to use that. Just a sherry, officer, maybe two. National
service reunion: get together with the boys; you know the
sort of thing. Should have remembered the pills, of course.
Trying a new treatment, for the migraine. Nasty business,
Malaya: nasty wound, too. Not much to talk about, really.
Lucky to have made it, so the doctors say; should have
warned me about the pills though, silly buggers. Terribly
sorry. Guarantee it won't happen again. That a Korea
ribbon? North Africa! Christ, now that must have been
a war. 'Course it won't happen again, officer. Solemn
promise.

Bit different now. Couldn't defeat the progress of science:
blow into the bag, pee in the bottle, blood smear under the
microscope and there you were, fucked without a kiss.

Charlie looked up, neck aching from the effort. To his
right, the bridge illuminations necklaced the Thames,
chokers of ambers and yellows and whites and reds.
Charlie blinked, trying to sharpen the blur. Too bright
to be Battersea Bridge. The Albert then. Shit: he'd done

12

it again. He peered across the road for confirmation and got it from the road sign. Oakley Street. Second time it had happened recently. Or was it the third? He couldn't remember; didn't matter anyway. Missing Battersea Bridge did. Probably easier to go back. Why bother? He wasn't going anywhere, not tonight. Or any other night. Charlie reached out for the support of the metalwork, swinging himself into position to cross the bridge for the roundabout route to his Battersea flat. The footpath ribboned away ahead of him and Charlie paused for a moment, breathing deeply like an Olympic athlete preparing himself for the run that would win the gold. The pavement cracks; that's all he needed, a line of pavement cracks. He started out, head forward again, left right, left right, the impact against the concrete hard beneath his heels.

Used this bridge a lot in the early days. Vauxhall and Lambeth too. Mattered then, to vary the route. Not just on foot either. Underground during the rush hour when there were people among whom he could get lost. Buses, too. And a taxi, when he'd thought there was something suspicious and needed care – a cautious, circuitous route, tensed for any back-street dodging.

Never suspicious any more. No one was chasing Charlie Muffin. Quite safe to have a few drinks. No worry about surveillance.

He jerked up suddenly, grimacing in half-remembered awareness. Confined space, easy to spot. So they'd be running parallel observation, maybe triangular, one behind, one in front and the other making the third point, on the opposite side of the road. Charlie turned awkwardly, stumbling as his foot edge missed the kerb. He snatched sideways, grabbing for the wall. Far behind, on the further side of the road, a couple meandered entangled in groping love. In front a girl was approaching, hobbled by a short, thigh-hugging skirt. A man strode past him, bowler purposefully slanted over his forehead, tightly furled umbrella striking the ground in time to his marched progress, like a parade sergeant's staff. Too dark and too quick to see the regimental tie, but there'd be one. Just like the pricks who took over the department and tried to get him killed. Screwed them, though. Sucked them up and blew them out in bubbles.

He frowned, trying to remember why he was standing in the middle of the bridge, with his back protectively against the parapet. Surveillance! Trying to observe the observers. He sniggered, conscious of the whisky fumes at the back of his throat. Still good enough to spot them, if they'd been there. Quite safe, he decided positively.

He pulled upright, to continue across the river, confronting the girl approaching him. The skirt was tighter than he'd first thought. And shorter. Wasn't wearing a bra either, he saw, conscious of the bouncing turmoil under the clinging sweater. A professional, judged Charlie, with a vague stir of interest. He tried quickly to guess how much money he had in his pocket, feeling the coin edges and attempting to count the notes, holding them unseen separately between his fingers. Difficult to tell. Maybe ten pounds. More likely five or six, where he'd counted twice. Should be sufficient for a short time. Charlie squared himself, ready for the approach. The girl detected the interest, slowing her walk. Then, quickly checking the traffic in both directions, she crossed the roadway, heading for Chelsea and a better class of client on the opposite side of the river.

'Fuck me,' said Charlie inappropriately. Once more he sniggered. No one wanted Charlie Muffin; not even whores.

Or Rupert Willoughby. The thought broke through the drunkenness and he stopped sniggering. The call to the Lloyds underwriter had been a gesture of desperation, the thing he'd tried to avoid after what had happened with Clarissa in America. Unavailable, the secretary had said. Bit different from his wife. The booze washed through him, flooding the reflection. Charlie resumed his stilted progress, left right, left right, guiding himself by the kerb rim when there weren't any paving stones, turning westwards at the far side of the bridge and retracing his path through the streets until he got to the tower block in which he hid, an ant among other ants. There were two bicycles fixed to the stair railings by a security chain and beneath the stairwell an abandoned pushchair, robbed of its wheels and squatting on its axle like the mother ant. There was a sour odour of dust and cabbage and paraffin. Someone had written 'It's me against the world' with an aerosol can across the far wall.

'Hope you win,' muttered Charlie. He hadn't.

The lift was broken, which was usual, so he stumped up the stairs, pausing at each floor, breath wheezing from him. His legs ached with the effort and, by the time he reached the fourteenth storey, he felt ill and sick. He reached out, supporting himself against the wall. It was several minutes before he could go through the linking door into his corridor. He stumbled on to the doorway, initially missing the lock with his key. Eventually inside, he slumped down, without taking off the plastic raincoat which hadn't been necessary anyway, because the forecast had been wrong and it hadn't even drizzled.

'Buggered,' he told himself. 'You're completely buggered, Charlie.'

It hadn't been so difficult, when he'd first gone on the run. Often climbed the stairs then, to check if anyone was following, ducking in and out of landings, ears strained for the sound of pursuit. He'd done other things too in the surveillance detection manual. Like leaving miniscule fabric placings around the door to detect entry, and examining the lock for minute scratches, and arranging books and shirts and pocket flaps in certain ways, so he would know if there'd been a search. And always leaving the window open to the fire escape, for immediate flight.

Then there had been a reason for it. Edith had been alive, sharing the existence and the fear, ageing visibly and trying to hide it. *'I didn't know it was going to be like this, Edith. But trust me. We'll beat the bastards.'* And so she'd trusted him, like she always had. But he hadn't beaten them. At the moment when it had mattered, when he thought the vengeance hunt had been abandoned, he'd relaxed. And the bullet meant for him had taken away half her spine.

Charlie shook his head, an angry, physical gesture. The recollections of Edith were in the closed, no-entry part of his mind, the place of the deepest guilt. Always came out when he drank too much.

15

Charlie struggled up, moving through the pot-cluttered kitchen, opening cupboards and then the refrigerator, staring disappointedly at the age-wrinkled tomato and some forgotten celery, limp like he would probably have been if the whore hadn't crossed the road. He'd meant to bring something back from the pub, but he'd forgotten: he seemed to forget a lot of things lately. Charlie groped back into the main room, staring around as if seeing it for the first time.

The home of the nobody man. There were no mementoes or souvenirs or photographs, not even of Edith. It was like a doll's house setting, which real people never occupied, a small settee and two matching chairs and a cabinet with some books he could never maintain the concentration to read and a television which bored him with its inanities. A place to come to, out of the rain, when the forecasters got it right.

Directly inside the bedroom, Charlie halted in near fright at the sudden, sag-shouldered reflection in the wardrobe mirror. He still wore the unnecessary raincoat and looked like a bundle that someone had been embarrassed about and tied in polythene before leaving on a rubbish dump. About right, he thought. He undressed, letting the clothes puddle about him on the floor, but ignored the bed. Charlie knew it would rise and fall on the sea of booze if he lay down, until he had to dash for the bathroom anyway. He filled the basin with water and sank his face deeply into it. He kept coming up for breath, then down again, finally panting to a halt and gazing at his dripping, pouch-eyed image. Broken veins showed bright in his nose and cheeks.

'Bloody fool,' he said. The whisky-buoyed bravado was ebbing away. They wouldn't have forgotten. Just one mistake and the hunt would start all over again. And he didn't want to get caught. Any life, even one as empty as that he now lived, was better than what would happen if they ever found him.

Charlie dried his face and was reentering the bedroom when the telephone which never rang jarred through the tiny apartment. His immediate reaction was one of fear. He watched it for several moments and then reached out hesitantly.

'Hello?' There was still a vague fog of alcohol in his voice.

'Charlie,' said the voice. 'I've been calling you for hours. It's Rupert Willoughby.'

Charlie had rehearsed the approach but when the time came he couldn't think of the prepared words. Instead, he said, 'I'd like to see you.'

'Good idea,' said the underwriter. 'I've got a bit of a problem.'

It was a measure of how careless Charlie had become that he talked unaware of the listening device that had been implanted in his receiver. In the early days he had dismantled it regularly, but, as with everything else, he hadn't bothered for months.

Sure of the man and his movements, they recrossed the river after the surveillance ended, because the pubs were better in Chelsea and Pimlico. They should not have gathered in a group at all, just as they shouldn't have left Charlie's apartment block until the arrival of the relief team, but they had been doing it for so long, on monthly rotating shifts, that most of the usual rules were being ignored. Tonight it was the pub on the corner of Bessborough Place. The supposed whore was first; the ridiculous shoes had made her feet hurt and she had managed to get a taxi. The two who had pretended to be lovers arrived as she was ordering the drinks. They went straight to a vacant table, waiting for her to carry the glasses across.

'Good health,' said the man, lifting the beer mug. His fingernails were bitten and he had chipped teeth; his breath smelled and the girl in the exaggerated high heels was glad she hadn't been selected to be his partner.

'Cheers,' she said. Beneath the table she slipped off the shoes and began kneading her feet. 'I actually thought he was going to approach me tonight.'

'What would you have done?' asked the man.

Knowing the answer would upset him, she said, 'Gone with him, of course.'

'It's been a year,' protested the other woman. 'It's stupid.' Crossing the bridge, her partner had touched her breast, twice, pretending it was an accident but she knew it hadn't been. She knew there was no objection she could make either. Dirty bastard.

'Difficult to imagine that he was once so good, isn't it?' said the man reflectively.

'I don't think he ever was,' said the girl in the prostitute's disguise. 'I think it's some typical bureaucratic mistake in Moscow; the sort of thing they do all the time.'

The man shook his head positively. 'Not this one. Charlie Muffin is important, for some reason.' He looked at his watch. 'We'd better get back to the embassy.'

The two women looked at each other, irritated. It was the third night in succession he'd avoided buying any drinks and they were sure he was charging more on his expenses than they were.

'This is a shitty job,' complained the girl who had been fondled. 'Really shitty.'

By the time they got back, the telephone conversation between Charlie and Rupert Willoughby had already been reported to Moscow. And Kalenin knew the protection he had evolved was possible. The priority cables were already arriving from Dzerzhinsky Square.

'I'm bored.'

Rupert Willoughby didn't bother to look up from his book at Clarissa's protest. 'As usual,' he said.

'Amuse me then.'

'I'm your husband, not your jester.'

'And fuck all good at either.'

'You really shouldn't swear,' said Willoughby. 'You always sound as if you're reading the words from a prompt card.'

'Fuck!' she said defiantly.

'Still not right,' said Willoughby, knowing the condescension would irritate her even more. He lowered the book to look at her. She was moving listlessly around the apartment, lifting and replacing ornaments and running her hand along the top of the furniture.

'Jocelyn and Arabella have taken the yacht to Menton,' she said.

'I know.'

'They've invited me down.'

'They usually do.'

'I thought I'd go.'

'Why not?' Intent on her reaction, he said, 'I'm seeing Charlie Muffin tomorrow.'

'Charlie!' She stopped. The brightness was immediate. 'I'd love to see him again.'

She'd tried hard enough after New York. Which is what had planted the idea in Willoughby's mind after the man's telephone call and the yacht invitation.

'I'll ask him to dinner,' he promised.

2

The office of the intelligence director was on the Waterloo side of the Thames. Sir Alistair Wilson asked the driver for the cross-over route through Parliament Square; purposely early for the meeting with the Permanent Under Secretary responsible for liaison between the department and the government, he'd heard the displays were particularly good this year and he wanted to see for himself.

The rose beds in St James's Park were by the lake, bursts of Ophelia and Pascali and Rose Gaujard. He leaned forward, studying with an expert's eye the colour lustre and feeling the texture of the leaves. Growing roses was Wilson's hobby and he liked to see a naturalness about their arrangement, not this patterned rigidity, as if they were sections of some jigsaw puzzle. But over-arranged or not, the blooms were better than his. It had to be the soil in Hampshire, full of chalk. When he got the chance, he'd talk to the gardener about increasing the compost to balance. Wilson smiled at the thought; he was going to do so much, when he got the chance.

Distantly, somewhere in the direction of the Mall, a clock bell chimed and he set off towards Whitehall. For a man who until five years before had commanded a Gurkha regiment and been seconded to intelligence with a reputation for efficient discipline, Wilson's appearance was a personal contradiction. Careless of the obvious amusement it caused within his working circle, he wore a deerstalker, because it had flaps he could bring down over his ears in the winter and after so much time in India he suffered from the cold. The suit was good but neglected, thick tweed – again for the cold

– but the trousers were absolutely without crease: although there were lots of the wrong sort, crimped tiredly behind the knees and elbows. The overcoat, of forgotten fashion, was too long and over-padded at the shoulders and cuffs, and again at the elbows the wear was obvious; in another six months, it would be threadbare.

He was bonily thin and the face was hawkish, big-nosed, with sharp, attentive eyes. Greying hair escaped from beneath the hat, like a plume, heightening the bird-like appearance. He moved awkwardly, limping where the left knee refused to bend. Wilson had come unscathed through Europe, Korea and Aden but almost lost his leg when a polo pony fell and rolled on him in Calcutta. For years it had irritated him, because of the physical hindrance, but now he was only aware of it in the coldest weather, when the ache settled deep in his calf.

After the confetti of memoranda and demands for speed, Sir Alistair knew that the location of the leak, coupled with the timing, would increase rather than diminish the pressure. It was like sailing out of the fog and seeing the rocks only yards away.

Sir Berkeley Naire-Hamilton hurried fussily across the office to meet him, hand outstretched. 'Good to see you, my dear fellow. Good to see you.'

'And you,' said Wilson.

'I've tea. Earl Grey, I'm afraid. All right? You'll take it with lemon, of course?'

The man bustled around a side table where the tea things were set, asking the questions automatically without any wish or expectation of a reply.

Wilson accepted his tea and, instead of returning to his ornate, over-powering desk, Naire-Hamilton seated himself opposite the director on a matching, wing-backed chair.

'Delighted to hear there's a breakthrough,' he said.

'I'm not sure you will be,' warned Wilson.

'What do you mean?' demanded the permanent civil servant. Naire-Hamilton was a florid-faced, balding man, a rim of tightly clipped white hair hedged around his face. There was the hint of a minor stroke or some facial paralysis, which had caused the left-hand side to collapse slightly, making one eye more pronounced than the other. Naire-Hamilton had a tendency to the flamboyant, with broadly striped suits and pastel shirts with matching ties. It went with the vague foppishness of the office. It was traditional Whitehall, like bowlers and striped trousers with black jackets and vintage Dow with Stilton. The furniture was predominantly Georgian, bulbous-calved with a lot of leather, and there were ceiling-to-floor bookcases with volumes that couldn't easily be removed because they'd remained unread for so long that the covers were stuck edge to edge. The walls were panelled and hung with portraits of bewigged chancellors and diplomats and there was a large and heavily decorated grandfather clock. It ticked with a constantly sticky, hesitating tick, demanding to be listened to in case it didn't reach the next second. Wilson found the clock irritating. He wasn't sure about Naire-Hamilton either.

'Rome,' announced Wilson.

'You can't be serious!' Naire-Hamilton brought his hand up over his sagging eye, a habit of embarrassment.

'I wish I weren't.'

'That's ... it's ... .' Naire-Hamilton's hand moved from his eye, in a snatching gesture, as if he could pick the proper expression from the air.

' ... where the traitor is,' said Wilson.

Naire-Hamilton carefully replaced his teacup on a wine table beside his chair and said, 'Tell me why you're so sure.'

'Four months ago we started transmitting in monitored batches through normal Foreign Office channels an apparently genuine advisory document, recommending the manner of British response to Russian efforts to increase its influence throughout Africa.'

'Why Africa?'

'Because we had a lot of embassies to cover and the size of the continent gave us sufficient number of towns and cities.'

'I don't understand.'

'The document was identical, but each message listed a different African city or town from which the intelligence prompting the cable was supposed to have come. And each receiving embassy was accorded an identifiable capital; the effect was to make each cable individual.'

'Jolly good,' said Naire-Hamilton. It sounded as if he were applauding the winning six during the annual Eton–Winchester cricket match.

'Three days ago the document was relayed from Moscow to all the Warsaw Pact embassies. Our source checked back with Prague, for clarification, as we instructed. And got the reply that the message emanated from Cape Town.'

Naire-Hamilton frowned but, before the question came, Wilson said, 'Cape Town was the code allocation we gave Rome. There can't be any mistake.'

'That couldn't be worse.'

'I thought it might be bad.'

The Permanent Under Secretary splayed his fingers, to tick off the points. 'In three weeks' time, Italy is hosting a Common Market Summit; every European president, prime minister, foreign minister and God knows how many other ministers will be there.... ' The first finger came down. 'Chief item on the agenda is an attack mounted by us against Italy, for using Market regulations to avoid their full budgetary contribution.... ' He lowered the second finger. 'We intend announcing our intention to lessen our financial commitment to NATO unless Italy gets into line.... ' Down went the third finger. 'This year Britain has the presidency of the Council.... ' He threw up his hands in despair. ' ... and now we're going to be shown up as the country to have right in the middle of everything a traitor leaking it all back to Moscow.... '

'I understand the difficulty,' said the intelligence director. Naire-Hamilton seemed to have overlooked that there had been three assassinations; perhaps he didn't have enough fingers.

'Discretion,' announced the civil servant.

'What?'

'It's to be handled with discretion: absolute and utter discretion. No scandal whatsoever.'

'We haven't got him yet,' said Wilson.

23

'There can't be any embarrassment,' insisted Naire-Hamilton.

Conservative parties, Labour parties and even Social Democratic parties might fight elections and dream of power, but people like Naire-Hamilton regarded the changes like a bus driver allocated a temporary inspector: there might be occasional changes of route, but they were always in the driving seat.

Wilson straightened in his chair and the leather elbow patches squeaked against the seat. 'Are you telling me you don't want a trial?'

Naire-Hamilton sucked at his breath, noisily. 'Just giving general guidance, my dear fellow. More tea perhaps?'

Wilson wished the other man wouldn't keep calling him a dear fellow. He shook his head against the offer. 'If there were an accident, you wouldn't regret not being able formally to endorse the file closed?'

'Admirably put,' congratulated the other man. 'And another thing.... '

'What?'

'I think it would be best if you remained in personal charge. Confusions always arise if things as important as this get delegated.'

'I hadn't any intention of delegating anything,' said Wilson.

'Glad to hear it, dear fellow,' said Naire-Hamilton. He raised his ever-moving hands against his forehead in a measuring gesture. 'Up to here with traitors and super-spies,' he said.

For some inexplicable reason, the Ministry of Works, which was responsible for government decoration, considered buildings south of the river to be modern, for which Wilson was grateful. There was the obligatory bookcase, with its stuck-together tomes, but otherwise he was spared Naire-Hamilton's working conditions. There were even two Dora Carrington pictures on the wall. The window view of the river included St Paul's and the furniture was sufficiently contemporary not to make the television set, on which

Wilson sometimes watched afternoon horse racing, appear obtrusive. Since the Calcutta accident, racing was the nearest he got to horses: once they'd been a hobby, like roses.

Peter Harkness was waiting when Wilson returned from his Whitehall meeting. The deputy intelligence director was an undemonstrative man whose initial training had been as an accountant and who still worried about money. He lived separately but beneath the same Bayswater roof with a wife to whom he had been married for twenty years and wouldn't consider divorcing because both were practising Catholics. Apart from church on Sundays, when he carried her missal, they were never seen together. She went to old-time dancing Wednesdays and Fridays, and at weekends, apart from church, Harkness sailed his radio-controlled model of the *Cutty Sark* on the Round Pond in Kensington Gardens. Even then he wore a hard-collared shirt and a waistcoat.

'What was the reaction?' asked Harkness.

'What I expected,' said Wilson. 'The instruction is absolute discretion.'

'I thought that went with the job.'

'No arrest or trial.'

'Oh,' said Harkness heavily.

'It makes good political sense,'

'What about moral sense?'

'Naire-Hamilton's morals are political.'

Harkness appeared about to challenge the assertion, but swallowed it back. 'We've still got a lot of phoney messages to go. Shall I withdraw them?'

'No,' said Wilson at once. 'People had to be involved at the Foreign Office: if we stop, they'll know we've got a lead. They might even identify it, by a process of elimination. I'm not risking another Philby situation, a protector back here at base.'

'All the Rome personnel files will be processed by tomorrow,' promised Harkness.

'We might get a lead,' said Wilson doubtfully. 'What about the embassy itself?'

'Completely isolated from anything sensitive.'

Wilson leaned back reflectively in his chair; again the

leather patches squeaked rudely. 'We've got an advantage there,' he said.

'What?'

'The Summit,' said the director. 'We can move a squad into the embassy, as supposed security for the meeting.'

'Any specific instructions?'

'Not yet. It's isolated, as you say. So there's no danger any more. The only risk is that our man might get nervous and run; a defection could create the sort of embarrassment Naire-Hamilton is frightened of.' Wilson swivelled his chair towards the window. Outside, a stacked jet, waiting for Heathrow landing permission, appeared to hover over the Houses of Parliament. 'What about Hotovy?' said the director suddenly.

'His two boys are here, in London. But his wife is undergoing some sort of medical treatment in Brno.'

'He won't cross without her?'

'No.'

'Damn!'

'He's been as exposed as hell for six months.'

'How long before she gets back?'

'A week he thinks.'

'There wasn't another way.'

'I know.'

'If his wife's back within the week, he's still got a chance.'

'Just a chance,' agreed Harkness.

3

Charlie Muffin took the better of his two suits from the cleaner's bag and laid it on the bed for comparison with the new shirt and tie; the trousers were still a bit shiny at the seat and there was a small fray at the turn-up on the left leg, but overall it was good enough. Poncy bugger, he thought, self-critically, conscious of the effort to impress. There hadn't been many times when he'd bothered. Marks and Spencer, 1959, he supposed. Trainee manager, £3 a week, subsidized canteen, two weeks' holiday a year and a guaranteed pension: his mother had a thing about pensions, just like she had about wearing clean underpants every day in case he was ever knocked down in the street. And the wedding, to Edith. Except that he hadn't managed it then. He'd meant to, like he'd meant all the promises he'd made to her. Just slipped his mind, in the pub. So he'd arrived at the registry office with the jacket of the new suit still damp from sponging away the spilled vindaloo of the previous night's stag party curry, a hangover that would have felled a bear, and had had to excuse himself halfway through the register signing to throw up in the vestry lavatory. Hadn't done that successfully either, so he'd reappeared with fresh sponge marks on the suit. Edith hadn't been lucky from the very beginning.

Charlie took the new suede brush and carried into the kitchen the Hush Puppies that age had moulded into some sort of comfort for his feet, buffing hard to bring up a better nap. He'd worn new shoes for the job interview and the wedding, but he couldn't now. Charlie Muffin had problem feet. Some days were worse than others. Today was bad. They were not misshapen or deformed or calloused: they just

27

ached most of the time. He'd placed them – cautiously – into the hands of chiropodists and specialists who recommended supports, arches, built-up heels, shaved-away soles, and finished up where he'd started, with aching feet.

Charlie thought he should have received a pension. They were awarded for hernias and other army disabilities. And he was bloody sure that's what he had – a provable disability from stamping around national service parade grounds in boots weighing a ton and over which they'd made him crouch, day after day, burning out the toecap lumps with a hot spoon and then polishing and spitting and polishing and spitting, to get a shine.

It was to escape from the parade ground that he'd sat the examination for the intelligence corps, competing with the Sandhurst failures who gargled their words and had MG sports cars to take advantage of the weekend passes they always seemed able to get. And beaten the bloody lot, with a 98 per cent pass mark, straight into a warm office and a comfortable chair. Which was all, initially, he'd considered it – a place to rest his feet and escape the stupidity of scrubbing coal bunkers with toothbrushes and soaping the inside of his trouser creases to keep them in shape for colonel's inspection.

It had come as a surprise to find that he liked it. And was good at it. Where two other investigations had failed, he'd managed the arrest in Vienna of a cipher clerk dealing directly with the Russians and been promoted sergeant, but even then it hadn't occurred to him that it might become permanent. After demob there was still Marks and Spencer and the guarantee of pension rights.

Three months before demob he'd been told, without explanation, to present himself to Whitehall, so he'd polished the boots and soaped the creases and gone anticipating some escort duty. And instead found himself in a high-vaulted, cavernous room confronting a committee of men who moved and spoke quietly, because things echoed and they seemed frightened of the noise disturbing the people next door.

They'd known everything about him. Not just what he'd

done in the army, which would have been easy enough from records, but before. They had the headmaster's reference and the Marks and Spencer personnel file; they actually knew what his mother had earned, charring, to keep him at grammar school in Manchester. He supposed they knew about the other thing too, the blank space on the birth certificate where his father's name should have been recorded. Cheeky buggers. He'd thought so at the time but said nothing. What they were offering appealed more than being a trainee manager and the pension terms had been better, so his mother was happy enough.

Life would have been a damned sight easier if he'd remained a disciple of St Michael, thought Charlie, going into the bathroom.

Charlie shaved delicately, to avoid cutting himself, not wanting to meet Rupert Willoughby with tiny flags of toilet paper all over his face. He wetted his hair to keep it in place, but used too much water and knew that when it dried it would stick up. It usually did, so there wasn't much he could do about it. Ready long before it was time to leave, he surveyed the completed impression, standing sideways and holding in his breath and stomach to hide the bulge. Dissatisfied, he turned full frontal, squaring his shoulders and stiffening his neck, as he had on the long-ago parade grounds.

'Christ!' he said.

Willoughby's office was close to the main Lloyds building in Lime Street. It was the sort of place that never changed. There was the same rickety, stubborn lift, models of boats in glass cases, scrolls of honour commemorating past chairmen and employees who had died in both wars, lots of dark wood everywhere and the smell of polish. Rich and enduring, thought Charlie; a million miles from a Battersea tenement where the kids thought aerosol sprays had been invented to write 'Fuck' on the walls. If they had to do it at all, it was better than 'Nigger', he supposed.

Charlie made his way along the familiar corridors to the receptionist, who smiled and said he was expected. Charlie tightened his stomach, secured the buttons of his crisply cleaned suit and pressed his hands over the straying hair; it was sticking up, like he'd feared it would.

'Good to see you again, Charlie,' said Willoughby. The underwriter, who was a tall man, and uncomfortable because of it, unfolded rather than stood from behind his desk.

The office was fittingly traditional. There was heavy panelling, again the pungent smell of polish, the model of a paddle steamer in a case and an almost soundless tape machine, spewing a tiny stream of information neatly into a special container.

'Good to see you too,' said Charlie. Guessing the reason for the frown that momentarily crossed the other man's face, Charlie added, 'Had a bad night.'

Willoughby thought it looked as if there had been a lot more than one. Charlie had always been unkempt but never careless. Willoughby suspected that the shabby suede shoes and department-store suits, pockets bulged with mysteries, had always been a contrived camouflage of anonymity behind which the man operated, using the condescension of others to his own advantage. The underwriter had never seen Charlie Muffin in a pressed suit or crisp shirt. There was an obvious inference and Willoughby was glad of it; if Charlie hadn't wanted employment, it might have been difficult.

'Sorry I didn't return your call earlier,' apologized the underwriter. 'I was out of town.'

'Thought it was time to make contact again,' said Charlie.

'Why did it take you so long?'

Because I screwed your wife in America and knew it would continue if I kept in touch, thought Charlie. He was sure, after so long, that Clarissa wouldn't be a problem any more. He said, 'Busy, with one thing and another.'

'That's good,' said Willoughby. He was a sparse, hesitant man of half-completed, hurried movements. Every few moments he brushed back from his forehead an imaginary flop of hair.

'I'm not any more,' said Charlie quickly.

The secretary came in, carrying a silver coffee tray, fully

laid; even the coffee pot and the jugs were silver. If Willoughby had had a po under his bed, that would have been silver too, thought Charlie.

Willoughby poured. Offhandedly he said, 'Thought about you a lot: Clarissa often asks after you.'

Charlie remained impassive. 'How is she?'

The underwriter settled back in his chair. 'Fine,' he said.

Charlie decided that Willoughby was nervous and wondered why.

'After what you did, it was *me* who should have called you,' said Willoughby abruptly. There was a surge of guilt and Willoughby reflected that it was a pretty shabby way of repaying someone who had prevented his going bankrupt over a phoney liner fire in Hong Kong or on the loss of a Russian stamp collection during the American exhibition. But then, if Charlie had done what he suspected, that was pretty shabby too.

'You talked of a problem on the telephone.' Charlie wanted to get to the purpose of the visit.

'Ever heard of Lady Norah Billington?'

'No.'

Willoughby was genuinely surprised. 'She's always in the newspapers,' he said.

'Not on the racing pages.'

'She's the Mendale heiress. There's an estate in Yorkshire, a villa in Jamaica, as well as Rome and a flat here in London, near us in Eaton Square.'

'What about her?'

'Her husband's got a lawyer's mind and reads the small print. A year ago I underwrote a replacement cover policy on her jewellery. It's coming up for renewal. First time value was one and a half million, but the indexed rise will bring it up to two million. I've got to agree the adjustment in writing and he's asked that I do so.'

'What exactly do you want *me* to do?'

'Guarantee the protection,' said the underwriter. 'It's listed in specific detail on the policy, but before I agree the rise I've the right to check the alarm system and the

31

protection. . . . ' Willoughby smiled. 'Father always said you were the most security-conscious man he had on the staff.'

That wouldn't be the assessment now, thought Charlie. The same bastards who set him up for sacrifice manoeuvred Sir Archibald's replacement as director, but Charlie knew the old man would never have condoned the retribution. *'Morals are important in an immoral business, Charlie.'*

When Charlie didn't reply immediately, Willoughby repeated apologetically, 'Not quite the sort of thing you did before.'

It wasn't, thought Charlie. Clerk's stuff. Senior clerk, maybe, but still a clerk. But it would be better than getting so pissed by nine o'clock every night that he couldn't count the bridges on the way home.

'I'd like to do it,' he said.

'Sure?' said Willoughby.

'Quite sure,' said Charlie. 'Where?'

'Rome,' said Willoughby. 'Sir Hector Billington is our ambassador there.'

Charlie felt an abrupt stomach emptiness, the sort of sensation that comes when a lift goes down unexpectedly. Seven years, he thought; nearer eight. Diplomatic turn-around averages three years, four at the most. He'd never been attached permanently to any embassy anywhere, just used the facilities passing through. And never Rome. What he'd done would have remained a secret, apart from those at the very top. So what was the risk? Less than 50 per cent. Acceptable enough, to lift himself out of the shit in which he'd been wallowing for too long.

'Fine,' he said. He'd just have to be careful and he'd always been that, until recently.

Willoughby put his hands flat against the desk top, in a tiny slapping motion. 'I've just had an idea,' he said.

'What?'

'Instead of checking through the files here, why not come to the flat tonight and look at them there? Then we can have dinner.'

The inclination to refuse was as always almost automatic. Then Charlie thought of warmed-up shepherd's pie, cardboard sandwiches and another empty evening in an anonymous pub.

'Sure Clarissa won't be inconvenienced by the short notice?' he said.

'Positive.'

As he passed through the outer office to the reluctant stop and start lift, Charlie was vaguely aware of a man in a grey-striped suit. He was reading a copy of the *Sun*.

Since the insistent instructions from Moscow, there was no longer any casualness about the observation; they'd even ignored the ABC café close to Willoughby's office, remaining instead in an alcove on the opposite side of the street.

The man who preferred night to day-time shifts, because there was more opportunity for accidental groping, spotted Charlie first.

'There!' he said.

The woman, shapeless in sweater, jeans and tennis shoes, let the man move out ahead of her, so there wouldn't be any body contact; if he attempted to maul her like he had all the others, she'd determined to kick him so hard in the crotch he'd wear his balls for a necklace.

4

General Valery Kalenin was an ambitious man who recognized the nearness of success and knew, without conceit, that he deserved it. For almost thirty years he had served the KGB faithfully, heading four of the five main directorates and leaving each better than when he had arrived. Latterly it had been the clandestine section responsible for overseas activities, and objectively he considered that branch of the Komitet Gosudarstvennoy Bezopasnosti more highly organized than at any time since its formation.

It was because of that pride that he instinctively opposed the assassination idea, when it was proposed by Boris Kastanazy. As an operation it was futile, a pinprick irritation disposing of men who would be immediately replaced. It was only after Kastanazy, anxious to reinforce his failing influence within the Politburo, had forced the decision through that Kalenin realized the possible advantage.

In a society of indirect conversations and sideways manoeuvring, it had been a positive gamble for Kalenin openly to oppose the scheme, arguing the danger of the Rome detection. There had been moments, in the initial weeks, when he'd regretted the outspokenness. But not any more. The purge had begun and, because of the stance he had taken, he was absolved from it. Kastanazy could be the only sufferer. Which meant a KGB vacancy on the Politburo.

Kalenin prepared himself carefully for the forthcoming encounter, knowing it was probably one of the most important of his career. He was a small man and aware of it, just as he would have been aware of the disadvantage of a speech impediment. To gain the impression of stature, he chose to wear his uniform and debated wearing the Order of Lenin and the Hero of the Soviet Union, eventually rejecting the medals as ostentatious. Ribbons would be sufficient reminder of the honours his ability had earned him in the past.

The driver's knock came precisely on time. Although he was ready, Kalenin delayed his response, unwilling to give any indication of anxiety: the man had other functions beyond driving, and Kalenin did not want any account of over-eagerness relayed. It was not until the third knock that he answered the door.

As always, the driver hurried out into the reserved central lane and Kalenin settled back in the deep leather seat. The final snows still clung defiantly, white in the chimney crannies and on the roofs, but black and traffic-gritted at the pavement edges and gutters. Helmeted babushkas, so swaddled in layers of cloth and rough-cut sheepskin that it was difficult to imagine a human body beneath the mushroom shapes, chipped and swept and gossiped at their brooms. In another month, thought Kalenin, it would be spring, the hills outside the city still wet but proudly green and with the new flowers under the birch and fir.

The signs said the grass should not be walked upon, so the Alexander Gardens were still white and obediently untrodden. The car passed the Tomb of the Unknown Soldier and the Monument to Revolutionary Thinkers and swept into the red-walled Kremlin through the Trinity Tower gate. There were already tourists, crocodiling through the museums and cathedrals to the right, where the public were allowed. There were a few foreigners, animated with cameras and brightly dressed. But the majority were Russian, bundled like the street cleaners and following their tour leaders with dull-faced, placid acceptance. Only the children appeared to be smiling, not seeming to regard the visit as an official comparison of past decadence with the improvements of the present. Why did Russians need vodka to make them laugh, thought Kalenin. That couldn't be anything to do with the past; they'd drunk as much under the Tsars as they did now. And under the Tsars had been allowed to fall down and freeze to death during winters like this. Now there were nightly street searches around the capital and sobering stations to which drunks could be taken and hosed back to sobriety.

The car turned left, towards the Senate and the cordoned-off area, cutting off Kalenin's view of the tourists. It was recognized as an official vehicle and gestured through towards the Praesidium wing. There was a guide waiting for him, which was unnecessary, but Kalenin fell into step with the procedure. How many times had he journeyed along these tall, echoing corridors, to appear before ambitious men and inquiring committees? Too many to remember. It would be good, to have others come to explain themselves to him. And it was going to happen, he thought confidently.

It was a room the Politburo used for committee meetings, away from the main, impressive chamber. All thirteen members of the Soviet hierarchy were assembled around the kidney-shaped table. Already there was a fug of cigarette smoke, with pushed-aside cups and glasses on the table; even an occasional loosened collar, he saw. Despite the impression of informality, there was a secretariat table at the side of the room with three stenographers as well as a technician to operate the tape equipment. Kalenin was glad there would be records.

Vladimir Zemskov, the First Secretary, was in the chair. He was a dried-out stick of a man, thin-haired and emaciated, like an erudite vulture. He was smoking – a full-packed, Western-style cigarette, not the half-and-half Soviet version – and when he spoke his voice was thick and phlegmy. 'There has been some preliminary discussion,' he said.

As he spoke, Zemskov looked sideways along the table, towards Boris Kastanazy. The man responsible for Politburo control of the KGB was a complete contrast to the First Secretary. Kastanazy was obesely fat, so much so that there was no impression of a neck, making it seem as if his head had been attached as some sort of afterthought. From the perspiration pricked out on Kastanazy's face, Kalenin guessed the open, damning criticism had already begun: Kastanazy looked as if he were gradually melting in the sun.

'I have no doubt that Rome has been exposed,' said Kalenin forcefully. He was aware of Kastanazy's facial expression, something like a wince.

'The embassy or the source?' queried Zemskov.

'It's too early to be positive,' said Kalenin. 'At the moment I think only the embassy.'

'Can it be saved?'

'I'm formulating proposals,' said Kalenin. 'The European Summit creates a difficult time limit.'

'We must have internal access to that conference,' insisted Zemskov. 'Decisions will be made affecting every one of our satellite borders in Europe. And not just Europe: Greece will be attending this year for the first time, so it's the Mediterranean as well. It's essential we know what happens.'

'It's precisely because of that importance that the British will want it settled before it begins,' reminded Kalenin. Heavily he added, 'And why the killings should not have been risked.'

'What do you propose?' asked the First Secretary.

'To let them.'

'What!' Zemskov's astonished reaction led the stir that went around the table.

'I'm going to give them what they're looking for,' announced Kalenin. 'Two, in fact. The British already regard one as a traitor: it'll make it easy for them to accept the other.'

'How long?'

'A week, I hope. A fortnight as the outside.'

'Which would leave more than a week to the Summit?'

'Yes.'

Zemskov coughed, an unpleasant sound. 'A great deal depends upon this, Comrade General.'

'I know,' said Kalenin.

Further along the table Kastanazy blew his nose, and quickly wiped his forehead. To Kalenin, Zemskov said, 'Proper gratitude will be expressed, for success.'

Kalenin showed no reaction to the promise for which he'd been hoping. Save Rome, and the seat would be his.

*

Igor Solomatin worked independently of the Soviet embassy in Rome, under false documentation and identity, and was sure he was undetected; but he still returned to Moscow by the prescribed dog-leg route, flying from Italy to Paris and then from Paris to Amsterdam, to pick up the Aeroflot connection to Moscow. He made the entire journey unaware of the rotating check squad of eight men instructed by Kalenin to act as his protection.

The man entered the spartan office at the rear of Dzerzhinsky Square respectful but not awed by his surroundings, and Kalenin was impressed: to be awed meant to be overly nervous and nervous people made mistakes. As close as he was to success, Kalenin was determined against any mistakes.

For more than an hour Solomatin sat attentively forward in his seat as Kalenin outlined the operation, the only movement an occasional nod. At the end Kalenin said, 'Well?'

'It should work,' said Solomatin.

Kalenin smiled, impressed again; most field operatives would have been fawning in their praise. He lighted a tubed cigarette and said, 'How is he?'

'Frightened,' said Solomatin.

'A lot rests upon him.'

'He recognizes that.'

'Can he do it?'

'I think so,' said Solomatin. 'What about the Englishman?'

'The flight reservations have been made. Once he's there, there's nothing he can do to avoid involvement. Are you sure of the Italian?'

'He's ready.'

Kalenin offered a file across the desk. 'There are all the details of the alarm system and burglar protection.... ' He stopped, at a sudden thought. 'He speaks and reads English, I suppose?'

'Sufficiently,' assured Solomatin.

Kalenin depressed the summons button on the desk intercom and said, 'Someone is returning to join those already with you in Rome. His name is Vasily Leonov.'

38

Solomatin turned, as the outer door opened. A slim, fair-haired man stood there. He wore Western-style clothes and there was about him a vague, almost distracted, attitude that Solomatin had known among professors at university. It was a fleeting impression, replaced at once by the suspicion that ground control of the operation was being taken from him.

'What's your function?' he demanded, ill-phrasing the question in the spurt of annoyance.

'I kill people,' said Leonov.

5

The conversion of the huge Regency mansion in Eaton Square made Willoughby's London home a duplex – servants' quarters and kitchens on the ground floor and a lift to the first where they lived overlooking the central park. The underwriter answered the ground-floor entry bell, instantly releasing the door, and Charlie entered into a polished marble hallway where nobody had ever dumped prams or bikes or left messages on the wall. There was a small vanity mirror in the lift and Charlie stared back at himself, deciding the flush was from hurrying across the square. Now that it was about to happen, his feeling at meeting Clarissa again was eagerness rather than apprehension. New York had meant nothing, he was sure; a between-the-sheets experiment which had worked because they were both good at it. He'd been a bloody fool to imagine it was anything more.

Quickly he tried to control the shank of hair that curtained his forehead and was still with the comb in his hand when the lift stopped. Hurriedly he pocketed it, glad no one was waiting directly outside.

The lift led out onto a small foyer. Willoughby was waiting by the open door into the apartment.

'Come in,' he said.

Charlie had visited once before but there had been a lot of people and he hadn't been aware of the size of the place. There was a large central corridor, with doors leading off either side; those into the drawing room were double-fronted and open, giving an expansive entry.

'Clarrisa's out,' said the underwriter, leading Charlie in.

'Got herself involved with some charity for abandoned animals.'

Charlie thought he made it sound a sudden hobby that would soon be discarded, like collecting train numbers or cigarette cards. 'You should have called if it was inconvenient,' he said.

'She wouldn't hear of it,' said Willoughby. 'And it gives us time to go through the insurance file.'

A man appeared at the door and Willoughby motioned him away. 'It's all right, Robert; I'll do it.' The underwriter came back to Charlie. 'Drink?' he said.

'Scotch,' said Charlie. He was glad Willoughby was wearing a lounge suit. On the way from Sloane Square underground Charlie had wondered if he were expected to dress: he'd hired a dinner suit the last time and kept being mistaken for someone brought in to help for the evening.

Willoughby handed Charlie the drink and said, 'I've got the stuff in the study.'

It was miniscule by comparison to the City office, but still opulent, red-felt walls, a small antique desk and chair, a soft light apart from the single anglepoise lamp, a storage bureau, roll-top and antique again, and some photographs. They were predominantly of Willoughby, at school and university, but then Charlie saw the wedding group and moved closer to it.

'Father used his influence and managed to get Westminster church,' said the underwriter. 'It was 1970.'

'I remember,' said Charlie. He had an operation to date it. Moscow: July. A randy MP crying foul because he'd been photographed with his trousers around his ankles with an Intourist interpreter looking irritated because she hadn't been able to take her suspender belt off for the camera. Charlie had done the only thing he could to reverse the scandal; exposed the silly bugger himself and made a fuss about entrapment of British politicians on a supposedly friendly trade visit. Charlie peered closer at the picture. This was how he would remember Sir Archibald. Cherub-faced and bright-eyed, like a garden gnome by a goldfish pond. Not like the last time, at Rye, after he'd been dumped: a food-stained, shaky old man, his memory so whisky-blurred that sentences never had a coherent ending. Next to Sir Archibald lounged Clarissa in a veil and engulfed in cascades of fashionable satin. Narrow-featured even then, high cheek-boned, her face chiselled by the permanent diet. Calorie-free tonic water for social appearances and hand-rolled cigarettes for highs, remembered Charlie. Did she still smoke or had that been a passing hobby, like stray animals?

'I've got the file here,' interrupted Willoughby.

Charlie turned back into the room, seeing for the first time the small chair that had been set for him alongside the desk. In front of the underwriter was a spread of documents and diagrams. Charlie took the side chair and twisted the lamp, needing the illumination in the shaded room. It was an extensive dossier, with illustrations of the protection system and lists of the jewellery indexed against individual pictures of each piece, taken from several different angles. The correspondence between the ambassador and Willoughby was included, together with biographies of Sir Hector and Lady Billington. It was thirty minutes before Charlie looked up.

'Wealth I ask not, hope nor love ... ' quoted Charlie. In the early days in the department he'd habitually made remarks like that, in a futile attempt to convey the impression of an education he didn't have.

'They're important people, Charlie.'

'I'll tug my forelock and keep my place,' promised Charlie. Sir Archibald wouldn't have made a point like that, even with cause.

'I didn't mean to offend you,' said Willoughby hurriedly.

'You haven't,' said Charlie. Why did people always suspect he'd break wind in a quiet moment?

They both started, surprised, when the study door burst open. Clarissa entered theatrically, opening her arms towards them. 'Darlings!' she said.

Both men stood. Charlie felt a pop of excitement, deep inside. She *hadn't* changed since New York. Even the hairstyle was the same, bubbled out and frothing to her shoulders, accenting the length and narrowness of her face. He'd forgotten the eyes and their startling blueness and the way

42

she accented that, too, limiting the make-up just to the palest lip colouring. She looked stunning.

'Charlie!'

Self-consciously, Charlie took her hands and kissed her lightly on the cheek.

'It's so *good* to see you!' she said.

'And you.'

'It's been *ages*!'

She still talked in italics. 'Yes,' he said.

The butler appeared at the door and Willoughby said to his wife. 'Do you want to change?'

'No.' She didn't even look at him. To Charlie she said, 'You've got fat.'

'The good life,' he said.

'What have you been doing with yourself?'

'This and that.' Charlie retreated behind the familiar cliché. The social difficulty, the impossibility of any normal, inconsequential conversation about the past week or the past month was what got to Edith first, before the fear. Despite an education which had ended in Switzerland and the time she'd worked before their marriage as Sir Archibald's secretary, which Charlie would have expected to widen her attitudes, Edith had remained the suburban woman. She liked dinner parties with neighbours and holiday photographs and gossip about children, even though they didn't have any themselves. *'We're dead, Charlie; we might as well go to Russia or the bloody moon. We haven't got a life any more.'*

'I'm working,' announced Clarissa proudly, offering her arm for him to go with her into the dining room.

'So Rupert said.'

She seemed to remember her husband. 'There was a committee meeting tonight and I've agreed to give a charity supper here.'

'If you like,' he replied.

'I like!'

Willoughby said nothing.

'Let's eat,' said Clarissa, coming back to Charlie.

The dining room was an unusual construction. Fifty people could easily have been accommodated, but there were

43

sliding partitions which criss-crossed in dividing positions, so areas could be closed off to suit the number of people to be seated. With only three, the room was reduced to an annex. A round table was set and Clarissa stood waiting for Charlie to help her to her chair. He held back for Willoughby to do it.

'It's a worthwhile charity,' said Clarissa to Charlie. 'You must come.'

'I'll try,' he said. He wouldn't. He was unsure even whether tonight was a good idea. Clarissa had always been dismissive of her husband but he hadn't suspected it would be this bad. He and Edith had never got like this, not even towards the end when there was every reason for the resentment and recriminations.

Under the butler's direction, a Latin-looking woman served pheasant, while he poured claret from a cut-glass decanter.

'Must be a year since you two were in New York,' said Willoughby.

'And two weeks,' added Clarissa. Charlie wished she hadn't.

'You must have enjoyed it there,' said the underwriter. 'Clarissa could hardly stop talking about it when she got back.'

'We did, didn't we Charlie? It was fun!'

'Fun' was a favourite word of Clarissa's, remembered Charlie. 'Yes,' he said. 'We had a few laughs.'

'Rupert doesn't laugh a lot, do you Rupert?' she said.

'I don't have much to laugh about.'

They'd probably squabble over whether every day began with a dawn, thought Charlie. He felt like a piece of rope, being yanked over a dividing line between them.

'Did you ever?'

'It seems a long time ago.'

'I can't even remember.'

'I don't expect much time for sightseeing,' said Charlie quickly. 'I'll only be away for two or three days.'

'No need to hurry back,' said Willoughby.

'What are you going to do?'

'Check the protection of some jewellery.'

'I'd forgotten,' said Clarissa, pushing her plate away practically untouched. 'That's what you did with Rupert's father, didn't you?'

'Not really,' said Charlie, side-stepping. 'I was more in administration: a clerk.'

She disregarded the qualification. '*Was* it like all the books?'

Charlie considered the question. No, he decided. In the books he'd read there was a beginning and a middle and a neat tidy end. Charlie couldn't remember many occasions when all the questions were answered and the uncertainties resolved, with the good guys winning and the bad guys losing. He'd always found it difficult deciding who were good and bad anyway. 'From where I was it seemed all paperwork and records and bureaucracy,' he said.

'Sounds dull.'

'It was.' He'd never thought it so. Trap or be trapped, trick or be tricked: the normal shitty chess game with too many sacrificial pawns.

'Charlie must still be governed by the Official Secrets Act,' warned Willoughby.

And liable under it for what he'd done to a maximum of fourteen years in jail, thought Charlie. He knew he couldn't be prosecuted under the Treason Act, because it had happened more than three years ago. Charlie had checked that in the reference section of Chelsea public library, between three o'clock pub closing and six o'clock opening.

'What's that supposed to mean?' demanded Clarissa.

'That we shouldn't embarrass him by asking questions.'

'For Christ's sake, Rupert!'

They were talking as if he weren't there, thought Charlie. The nobody man again; it didn't upset him. Another course was changed and with it the wine. Charlie sipped appreciatively: it had been decanted like the first but he wasn't good enough to identify it.

'Rupert has always been in awe of his father,' said Clarissa, including him at last.

'So was I,' said Charlie, irritated at her posturing.

Silence frosted around the table and Charlie tried to think of something to say. Then he thought, sod it. If they wanted to behave like spoiled kids, it was all right with him. The pheasant had been just as he liked it, not too high, and the ubiquitous Robert was always at his elbow with the decanter. He'd have a better class of hangover tomorrow.

'Have you finished your business?' demanded Clarissa.

'Yes,' said Willoughby.

'So you don't expect the rigmarole of port and cigars?'

Willoughby looked inquiringly at Charlie, who'd never been to a dinner where women withdrew. 'Whatever you prefer,' he said.

'I prefer you to come with me,' she said.

Charlie walked with her into the drawing room. The curtains were undrawn and there was just sufficient light to show up the silhouette of the trees. As soon as they entered, Willoughby said, 'Damn, there isn't any brandy.'

'Call Robert,' said Clarissa.

'He's downstairs: quicker if I get it myself.'

Clarissa turned as her husband left the room. 'Hello Charlie Muffin,' she said.

'Hello.'

'It's nice to see you again.'

He felt another stir, the feeling he'd known earlier. 'And you,' he said.

'Why didn't you call?'

'I didn't think it was a good idea.'

'Why not?'

'You know why not.' Charlie looked towards the large doorway through which Willoughby had gone. 'What the hell's wrong with you two?'

'Just normal.'

'That's not normal.'

She made an uncaring gesture. 'Your number's not in the book. I looked.'

'Why don't we leave it as it was, Clarissa?'

'How was that?'

'A novelty thing – the dustman and the duchess.'

'Is that how you thought it?'

'Didn't you?'

'No,' she said, all the brittleness of the evening gone. 'I'm surprised you did.'

There was a sound from the corridor and Willoughby reappeared, the refilled brandy decanter in his hand. 'Sorry about that,' he said.

He poured large measures into three balloons and handed them round.

'Here's to a successful trip,' he said.

'Can't imagine it being anything else, can you?' said Charlie.

'I hope not,' said the underwriter.

It had been a mistake to accept the invitation, Charlie decided, walking back towards Sloane Square. He still fancied her rotten and she knew it. He wouldn't see her again.

Clever though it had been, the British entrapment had a flaw and Kalenin seized it. Albania and Yugoslavia were not included in the list of countries to which the damning advisory message had been sent. Which left six. To the foreign ministries and the intelligence services in Warsaw, East Berlin, Prague, Budapest, Bucharest and Sofia he sent demands for any inquiry which had come back from any embassy, once it had been relayed. Kalenin was using the English plan in reverse. It shouldn't take long; it was very clever, after all.

6

Between his office and that of his deputy there was a room formerly occupied by someone with the title of Forward Planning Executive, which Sir Alistair Wilson properly regarded as a piece of bureaucratic nonsense and abandoned after his appointment. It was here that he and Harkness created their incident room, bringing in document benches, filing cabinets for analysis folders, and three progress boards on easels to chart the direction of the inquiry. The conference was scheduled for ten and Harkness entered as the clock was striking, dossiers parcelled on his outstretched arms. He dumped them on the prepared table and looked without expression towards the intelligence chief.

'Well?' demanded Wilson.

'Potentially bad,' said Harkness. 'Rome had grade two listing on the access list. I've gone back three years. If he's been leaking that long, Moscow has virtually been sitting in on most of the cabinet discussions affecting Europe. And, because of NATO, there's a lot of cross referencing with America.'

'So Naire-Hamilton's right about the possible embarrassment?'

Harkness hesitated, conscious of how the Permanent Under Secretary wanted the matter resolved. Reluctantly he said, 'Yes. We'd look very stupid.'

'Damn!' said Wilson.

'It's only an estimate,' qualified Harkness. 'He might not have been operating that long.'

'Or it might have been longer,' said Wilson objectively. 'Until we get him and can fix the date, I don't think we should minimize what might have happened.' He looked towards the records Harkness had brought with him. 'Any possibilities?'

'Two,' said Harkness.

'On what grounds?'

'Moscow service, when they might have been turned. One is our Resident in Rome.'

'Who'd have personnel movement access?'

'Yes.'

'Him first,' said Wilson.

Harkness took up the file, going to the second table so he could spread out the information. Before he began talking he pinned an official-looking, posed photograph to the first blackboard: the picture showed a heavily built, jowly man, with fair hair and a clipped, military moustache.

'Henry Walsingham,' said Harkness. 'Late entrant, after army service with the Green Jackets. Bought himself out at the rank of lieutenant. Tried a year with his father's broker-age firm in the City, then took the entry examination. Average pass. Went to electronic surveillance at the govern-ment communication HQ at Cheltenham and did well: sort of mind that understands technical things. Transferred back to secret intelligence eight years ago. High Commission in Canberra, where he met his wife. Tokyo, then Moscow. After Moscow he went to Washington. Left there about a year ago for Rome.'

'Record?'

'Average. There's a commendation for the way he handled a currency fiddle being run by some of the marines on security duty in Moscow, to avoid a scandal. Got them posted back here for a discreet court martial, which pre-vented the Russians getting upset.'

'Could have brought him to their attention, if they'd been investigating it as well,' suggested Wilson.

'Yes,' agreed the deputy.

'What about the Australian wife?'

'Name's Jill,' said Harkness. 'Enjoys parties, described as a popular woman.'

'Marriage happy?'

49

'They spent three months apart when he was posted to Tokyo: stated reason was that her mother was ill in Canberra.'

'Was that confirmed?'

'No,' said Harkness. 'I've already cabled for the inquiry to be made.'

'Money?'

'Only what he earns. The bank records will be here tomorrow.'

Wilson went closer to the blackboard, gazing at the personnel photograph for several moments. 'Who's the other one?' he said, turning away.

Again Harkness pinned a picture on the board before he started talking. This time it was of a smaller-featured, darker man, heavily bearded. He was staring intently and unselfconsciously towards the camera.

'Richard Semingford,' listed Harkness. 'Career diplomat. Father's a colonel, so the boy went to Stowe but didn't seem to fancy a military career. Modern history at Cambridge, graduated with a Second. Married an undergraduate there. Entered the Foreign Office with an average pass mark. Good record as trade counsellor in Washington. Initial secretaryship in Tokyo, at the start of the trouble over Japanese car imports, and did well. Three years in Moscow: distinction rating when he left. Posted to Rome eighteen months ago as Second Secretary. Regarded as promotion material and likely to get an ambassadorship if he doesn't make any sort of major mistake.'

'Wife?'

'Ann. Bank manager's daughter, from Henley-on-Thames. Archaeology buff, so she couldn't be more content in Rome.'

'Any marriage problems?'

'No suggestion of any.'

'Excessive spending?'

Harkness shook his head. 'No inherited money, from either side, but they seem to live within his salary and allowances. Two kids at boarding school back here, but the government pays for that, of course.'

'Bank records?'

'Here tomorrow, with Walsingham's.'

Wilson turned away from the tables, limping to the window. The view wasn't as good as from his office, just a foreshortened outlook of the Houses of Parliament and Big Ben.

'It's not much,' he said. It was an observation, not a criticism.

'No,' admitted Harkness.

'How many more at the embassy?'

'About forty, not including cleaners and transport staff; and I think we can reduce that number, if these two show up clean. The leak is obviously high, someone with maximum security clearance.'

'What about surveillance teams?'

'In place by tonight,' said Harkness. 'I've notified the embassy officially that six were coming to check security for the Summit. There's twelve they won't know about.'

'Walsingham and Semingford then,' said the director. 'It's a start at least.'

'The more detailed check might throw something up about them,' suggested Harkness, conscious of the other man's reservation.

'What about Hotovy?' said Wilson.

'He's maintaining contact,' said Harkness. 'There's still no news of his wife's returning from Czechoslovakia.'

'He's going to have to decide soon.'

'That's the trouble,' said the deputy. 'He already has.'

The theatrical flamboyance of the Garrick suited the Permanent Under Secretary, decided Wilson, following Naire-Hamilton from the bar along the corridor lined with original Gainsboroughs and Reynolds into the dining room. On the way the intelligence director recognized two stage knights and a millionaire novelist whose last book he'd attempted and found incomprehensible. It had been a spy novel.

The wine had already been decanted and as they sat Naire-Hamilton said, 'Claret, dear fellow. That all right with you?' He was in broad chalk stripe again. Today there

51

was a handkerchief in his top pocket – an almost perfect match for the pink carnation.

'Of course,' said Wilson.

'Like this club,' said Naire-Hamilton. 'Belonged for years. Lowered the standards a bit recently ... admitting women, things like that. But I still enjoy it.' His butterfly hands fluttered around, summoning waiters.

Wilson had a soldier's lack of interest in food and ordered liver because it was the first thing he saw on the menu. The Permanent Under Secretary went into debate with the head waiter before selecting the steak and kidney pudding. It came off the trolley and Naire-Hamilton made the man adjust the portion, increasing it, before it was served.

Conscious that they could still be overheard, Wilson said, 'Interesting paintings.'

'All genuine,' said Naire-Hamilton. 'Committee can't afford to insure the damned things, so we photograph them and hope they're too well known to be stolen.'

Their food was served and, when the waiters left, Naire-Hamilton said, 'What's the progress?'

His food forgotten, the intelligence director outlined the potential harm the traitor could have caused if he had been operating any length of time.

'That's appalling,' said Naire-Hamilton.

'It could be,' agreed Wilson.

'Rome's isolated now?'

'Absolutely.'

'I was summoned by the Foreign Secretary yesterday,' disclosed Naire-Hamilton. 'There's been discussion in cabinet committee. They're extremely concerned.'

'I'm not surprised.'

'The attitude was as I predicted,' said Naire-Hamilton.

Wilson didn't believe any cabinet committee would have been as direct as that, even for records that weren't going to be public for fifty years. Naire-Hamilton took a lot upon himself. 'I understand,' he said.

'The Summit is in three weeks,' continued Naire-Hamilton, pressing the argument. 'It's got to be over by then; can't have half the government entering the sort of situation we know to exist there. The Prime Minister is going to be using the embassy, for God's sake.'

He stared around the dining room to locate the trolley man. Wilson declined a second portion. Naire-Hamilton waited until he had been served, tipped the man 10p and said, 'You can take what I've said about the cabinet committee as a direct instruction.'

Wilson said, 'Shouldn't we find out exactly what's been happening before making arbitrary judgments?'

'Pretty obvious what's been happening.'

'Not to me it isn't.'

Naire-Hamilton carefully put down his knife and fork. Leaning forward he said, 'There isn't a choice over this.'

'Perhaps one might have to be made.'

'Three weeks,' insisted the Permanent Under Secretary. 'That's all you've got.'

The Soviet surveillance group followed Charlie from Battersea to London airport and reported within minutes of the flight departure, allowing Igor Solomatin three hours to get his people in position for the arrival in Rome. Four independent observers were waiting when Charlie emerged from the baggage reclaim area of Leonardo da Vinci airport. The photographs had been extensive, so they would have recognized him easily enough, without the added advice from London that his suitcase was secured as a precaution with string. Charlie considered the airport bus, knowing he would make at least £6 profit on his expenses account against a taxi fare, but decided against it; his feet hurt and he couldn't be bothered with the delay at the city terminal.

Willoughby's office had reserved him a room at the Grand Ville, on the Via Sistina. It was just two streets away from the Eden; even with the detour because of the roadworks, the distance was not more than four hundred yards. It was into the Eden that the British security team were booked.

7

Ostia has been the seaside for Rome since the days of the Caesars and the Billington villa occupied a site where a general serving under Claudius had lived. It was secluded from the other constructions along the coastline, the nearest neighbour at least a mile away. The highway looped along the red clay and granite cliffs, with a sheer drop into the sea on one side, and then turned sharply at a minor peak. And there, set out as if for admiration in the small valley below, was the mansion. It was built right against the cliff edge and, before the car began to descend, Charlie had a bird's eye view of a verandah, colonnaded and heavy with grapevines and bourgainvillea overlooking the sea. There were walls on the remaining three sides and Charlie was able to make out the central courtyard around which the main house was arranged. It was almost all single-storey, with just one upper level; five bedrooms, according to the insurance information. There was a fountain, with a figure motif he couldn't distinguish, directly in front of the gravel drive, and along its entire length there was a border of neatly barbered cypress trees. The gardens were tiered down to the perimeter fence, against which were regimented groves of olives and oranges and more wine grapes.

'Posh,' judged Charlie, as he slowed the car at the gate lodge. Charlie gave the name of Willoughby's insurance firm and noted, for the report he had later to prepare, the care with which it was scrutinized against a visitors' sheet by a uniformed security guard. As he was waved through he saw the telephone being lifted, to warn the main house.

Inside the grounds it was easier to see the cat's cradle of

electrical wiring topping the walls. There were electrical booster points at the corners and Charlie assessed the conduit weight powerful enough for a current that could kill. The cypresses were bigger than they had appeared from the approach road, shadowing the drive almost completely from the mid-morning sun. The protection ended just before the front of the house, and the sudden glare was disconcerting. Charlie squinted against the brightness, aware of a woman waiting for him. She came forward as he got out of the car, hand outstretched.

'I'm Jane Williams,' she said. 'Secretary to Lady Billington.'

Charlie was conscious of her aloof scrutiny. It had been hotter that he'd expected on the drive from Rome and his suit was concertinaed. He pulled at the sleeves, trying to straighten them and dry his hands at the same time. She permitted the briefest contact.

'Lady Billington asked me to look after you.'

Charlie grinned. 'What does that mean?'

Her face remained blank. 'It means I'll conduct you through whatever sort of examination you wish to make of the security precautions of the house.'

Squire's daughter, judged Charlie: twin-set, pearls and the hunt on Sunday. Except that because of the heat it was voile not cashmere and if she had to work for a living he didn't expect the pearls were genuine. She probably still rode, though. She was slim and small-busted, with a full-lipped, heavy-browed face. Her dark hair was strained back into a businesslike bun at the nape of her neck and the tortoiseshell spectacles were held like a wand of office in her hand. A fashion magazine image of the perfect secretary, he thought.

'Lady Billington suggests you join her for sherry later,' said the girl.

'All right,' accepted Charlie. He noticed that the fountain motif had water coming out of a cherub's nipples.

The secretary led the way into the villa through a side door. Charlie felt the chill of air conditioning and saw that the windows were tinted against the sun, in addition to the venetian blinds. The floor was black and white marble, like a chessboard, and halfway down the corridor there was another fountain. This time the water was spurting from a fish's mouth. There were recesses and alcoves with plinths and urns, and from them trailed tendrils of evergreen plants. She stopped at the beginning of the corridor that seemed to run the length of the house and said, 'What exactly is it that you want?'

'Reassurance, I suppose,' said Charlie. 'To know that the security is still good.'

'Sir Hector is very security conscious,' she said curtly.

'So it would seem. Is that electric circuit on the wall operated every night?'

'By a time switch,' she confirmed. 'It prevents human error, someone forgetting. There are floodlights, too, along the beach.'

'What about the house?'

'Why don't you see for yourself?'

There were restraining fixtures on the majority of the ground-floor windows, preventing their being opened more than six inches. There were two sets of French windows, one at the side overlooking the seaview verandah and the other at the front of the house, leading out onto the wide driveway. On each were two sets of breaker points, to sound an alarm if contact was interrupted. In addition there were pressure pads beneath the carpeting. The same protection was installed at all the doors. There was the main entrance, the minor door through which they'd come into the house, one leading out through the kitchen and a fourth out onto the verandah, separate from the French window. Charlie followed behind the secretary from place to place, checking the details against the protection listed upon the file copy he had brought from London.

'Are these manually activated?' he asked, testing her.

'Time switch again,' she said.

'But you can override it if you want to?'

'Of course.'

'Shall we see?'

'Whatever for?'

'To guarantee it works.'

'Why?'

'I would have thought that was obvious.'

'We weren't advised this would be necessary.'

'I've only just decided it is. Bells that don't ring aren't an awful lot of good, are they?'

'These work.'

'Have you tested them?'

She moved her feet, uncomfortably. 'No.'

'So we'll check, shall we?'

'But people will have to be warned: one alarm sounds directly into the local police station.'

'You'd better warn them, hadn't you?'

'Are you sure it's necessary?'

'Positive.'

She turned on her heel and flounced out, leaving him in what he supposed was a drawing room. Over the marble fireplace, the unspeakable in hunting pink pursued the unseen uneatable. The English scene seemed curiously out of place among the classical ornaments and carvings, which Charlie supposed were genuine. There was no sense that anyone ever visited the room except to dust. He ran his finger along the top of a side-table. They did that well enough. It was fifteen minutes before Jane Williams returned.

'Are you ready?' she said.

'If you are.'

Her face was expressionless. 'What do you want?'

'Is the alarm set?'

'Yes.'

'The police warned?'

'Yes. I told them we'd be testing for an hour and they were to ignore it during that time.'

Charlie went to the main entrance, first triggering the alarm by opening the door and then by stepping on the pressure pad. On both occasions, the alarm jangled piercingly. He repeated the process at every other entry point and at the French doors. The protection operated every time.

'Good,' he said.

'I told you it worked.'

'So you did.'

'Can I put the system back to automatic now?' There was a note of weariness in her voice.

'What about upstairs?'

'What about it?'

'Aren't there alarms?'

'You know there are.'

'Then they'll have to be tested, won't they?'

She marched off, with Charlie close behind, enjoying the bum movement beneath the skirt. Whoever followed Jane Williams up the stairs in different circumstances was a lucky sod, he decided. She turned abruptly and Charlie tried to clear his face of expression.

'Something the matter?' she said.

'No,' said Charlie. 'Nothing.'

They went first to the guest bedrooms. Sash bolts stopped the windows from opening more than six inches: the air conditioning made sense, Charlie realized. It seemed a great deal of trouble to go to, just for the pleasure of wearing shiny stones.

'Now the master bedrooms,' said Charlie.

'It seems an intrusion.'

'That's what burglars do,' said Charlie. 'Intrude.'

For a moment her control slipped, her face clouding. Quickly she recovered and said, 'Which one?'

'Your choice,' said Charlie, careless of the annoyance he was causing her. It was clear that in the staff social structure Jane Williams put him somewhere around the rank of boot black.

There were two doors at the head of the staircase and she went to the one at the right. 'Sir Hector's,' she said.

Charlie stopped just beyond the threshold. The furniture was heavy and masculine, appearing oddly out of place in a villa in the sun, wardrobes as well as the bureau and bed fashioned from solid, black teak. Near the dressing table there was a bust of a man whom Charlie presumed to be the ambassador, mounted on a slender marble plinth and to the side was a spotlight, angled to illuminate it. Above the bureau and continuing around the walls were framed diplomas of Billington's progress in life and there were a lot of photographs, from school group pictures, up through childhood to adolescence. There were several of a youth in shorts and cap, with a racing boat behind. Directly above the bureau a rack held the sawn-off blades of oars. Charlie moved closer. There were several groups with the sculls in the foreground and the crews with their arms around each other with the tactile need of sportsmen.

Jane Williams said, 'Sir Hector got a blue for rowing at Oxford.'

Charlie nodded towards the plinth. 'Shouldn't there be a laurel wreath?'

'It was sculpted by Sir Mortimer Wheeler,' she said.

'Gosh!' said Charlie.

Her face twitched at the mockery. 'The windows are there,' she said, pointing.

One set opened onto a verandah with a spectacular view of the sea. Chairs were arranged around a canopied table on which lay some binoculars. There were breaker points, similar to those on the floor below, and under-carpet pads again. The four other windows in the room were small; two had securing fixtures and two breaker alarms. He tested each one and every time the bells clanged out.

'There's a dressing room, where the safe is,' said Charlie, remembering the plans he'd studied with Willoughby.

Jane Williams went across the room to a linking door. The dressing room was strictly functional and predominantly feminine. Two walls were occupied entirely by cupboards, except for a small bureau, and along the third had been fitted an elaborate dressing table, complete with a light-surrounded mirror. Brushes, combs and hand mirrors were set out in an orderly pattern and the jars of creams and lotions were grouped together, like cuckoo's eggs in a nest.

In front of the only window was a chaise longue and a small table. Charlie moved around and raised the venetian blind. The glass was reinforced solidly into the frame, not to be opened. Charlie tugged at the cord to lower the blind and turned apologetically. 'I never can make these things work,' he said.

Sighing she jerked at the string, releasing it first time.

'Must be a knack,' said Charlie, enjoying her closeness. She stepped back hurriedly.

'Now I suppose you'd like to see the safe?' she said.

'I'm going to need Lady Billington for that,' said Charlie.

'What!'

'The jewellery check has to be completed with the owner.'

'But that's not convenient.'

'Neither is losing it.'

'Lady Billington has an appointment in Rome in. . . . ' She hesitated, glancing at her watch. ' . . . just under two hours. How long will it take to go through the list?'

'As long as it takes,' said Charlie unhelpfully. 'Certainly longer than two hours.'

'This really is most inconvenient.'

'She couldn't cancel Rome?'

'Of course not.'

'Then I'll have to come back.' Charlie wasn't upset at the prospect. It had taken a year for Willoughby to consider using him again and, like a child saving the strawberry in the pudding until last, he was in no hurry to rush it.

'I'll see what can be arranged,' said the secretary.

'We haven't examined Lady Billington's bedroom yet,' reminded Charlie.

Jane Williams opened the door, letting him precede her into a pink and white room of silk festoon blinds and tufted carpet. There was a four-poster bed, draped with Venetian lace and haltered at each corner by wide bands of pink silk. The walls were lined with silk too.

'It's like walking across the top of a wedding cake,' said Charlie. As he crossed towards the windows he was conscious again of photographs – a montage of Lady Billington, as a young child, in a horse-drawn carriage before a house large enough to be a palace, and then, older, on a ski slope with a villa behind her. There were pictures of her in yachts, cars, boarding aeroplanes and at receptions with the famous. Charlie recognized the Kennedys and the Rainiers. Why was it that the rich needed so many reminders of their privilege?

'Quite an album,' he said.

Jane Williams didn't reply.

There was a verandah matching that of the other bedroom, with a set of windows opening onto it. The protection was the same and the bells sounded the moment they were tested. The two additional windows had restricted opening.

'Satisfied?'

'You mentioned sherry,' said Charlie.

She looked at her watch again. 'I don't imagine Lady Billington expected it to take this long.'

'Why don't we see?'

The stairs were wide enough for them to walk abreast and this time she kept level, unwilling for him to follow her. All the way down the corridor she stayed in step with Charlie, until they reached a leather-padded recessed door. She knocked but didn't bother to wait for an answer.

'The insurance man,' she announced and Charlie conceded victory to her. The one who'd called every week on his mother in Manchester for the penny policy was flat-capped, bicycle-clipped and always had his hand ready for a tip.

Lady Billington smiled a smile that didn't falter at Charlie's crumpled appearance.

'How nice of you to come,' she said, as if he'd accepted a late invitation to make up a dinner number. Charlie guessed Lady Billington was about fifty but she didn't look it. She was heavy-busted, which was unfortunate because it unbalanced the slimness of her figure. She was brave enough to leave the slight greyness in her auburn hair, which was long and looped to her shoulders. And she didn't make the mistake of too much make-up. She wore a plainly cut dress, silk, which seemed to be her favourite material, and from the list that Willoughby had given him Charlie knew the pearls, which were matched to perfection, had been valued a year earlier at £17,000. The diamond brooch was real too: £10,000. Charlie was conscious of movement around her feet and saw two fluff-balls of cats. Angora, he thought. No, that was rabbits. Persian perhaps. He felt the irritation begin at the back of his throat.

'I said sherry,' remembered Lady Billington. 'But I prefer gin. What about you?'

'Scotch please,' said Charlie.

'Shouldn't do it, you know,' she said.

'Do what?'

'Drink in this climate; the Romans always watered their wine, but then look what happened to them.'

Charlie liked her. Lady Billington was the Rolls Royce to Jane Williams's Daimler, he decided, accepting the drink from the returning secretary. His nose was itching.

'Cheers,' said Lady Billington.

'Cheers,' said Charlie.

'Must have been an awful nuisance for you, coming all the way from London.'

'It was necessary for the valuation adjustment,' said Charlie, hoping that was the way proper insurance men spoke.

'Hector fusses so!' she said. 'Half the time people don't know the difference between the real thing and paste.'

'I'm afraid it's not finished,' said Jane Williams. 'It seems you have to be personally present when the jewellery is checked.'

'Whatever for!'

'You're the owner,' said Charlie. 'I can only accept proof of identity from you: it's a term of the policy.' He sneezed, just getting the handkerchief to his face in time.

'Can't do it today,' said Lady Billington. 'Due in Rome for lunch. Hector treats lateness as a diplomatic incident.' She was sitting on a wide couch. The cats snuggled up beside her and she began to fondle them.

'Your secretary explained,' said Charlie. 'I'm sorry. I should have explained on the telephone.'

'No matter,' said Lady Billington. She frowned at her empty glass and offered it to the other woman. 'And look at the diary, will you?'

She came back to Charlie. 'What *have* you done?'

'Checked the security, which was the main point of the visit,' said Charlie. 'It seems extremely efficient.'

'I heard the bells.'

Charlie realized she had a tendency to over-stress her sibilants and was unsure whether it was an impediment or the gin. 'From what I've seen I should think you're safe enough.' He sneezed again.

'Have you got a cold?'

Charlie looked towards the cats. 'Bit asthmatic,' he said. 'Reaction to animal fur.'

Jane Williams returned with the drinks and the appointments diary. Lady Billington held up the animals. 'Take them out dear, will you?'

Sighing, the secretary carried both animals out into the corridor. She returned picking fur from her skirt.

'Thank you,' said Charlie.

She said to Lady Billington. 'You could fit it in tomorrow.'

Charlie thought she made it sound like agreeing to a hack being shod.

'Come for sherry,' invited Lady Billington, sipping her gin.

The cats were clustered at the door, awaiting readmission when he left. Jane Williams showed him out. At the drive, Charlie said, 'See you tomorrow.'

'I doubt it,' she said, determined upon the last word.

Charlie sneezed, not managing the handkerchief in time.

Alexander Hotovy had stressed his wife's health when he made the request and had been given permission to travel to London airport to meet her on her return from Czechoslovakia. He sat in the rear of the car, confident neither the driver nor the escort who accompanied him would discern the excitement that was throbbing through him. It wouldn't be so easy with Lora: his wife knew him too well. He'd rehearsed the whispered warning for when they embraced, so she would not question him until they got somewhere secure to talk. Dear God, he prayed, let her be well enough to accept it without challenge. In a day – two at the most – they would all be safe.

The vehicle circled the roundabout and sped beneath the huge welcoming sign above the tunnel leading into the airport. Hotovy smiled at it briefly. That's what he was being welcomed to: a new life. A new life without restrictions or suspicion or worrying about an indiscreet word or thought. Freedom! His hands were wet with sweat. He took a handkerchief from his pocket and wiped them under the pretence of blowing his nose.

Safeguarded by the CD plates, the car parked on the double yellow lines outside the European arrivals building and Hotovy got out. He walked with deliberate slowness into the terminal, staring up at the indicator board for the flight from Prague.

'You are Comrade Hotovy?'

'Yes,' In his surprise, Hotovy answered before he realized that the question had been asked in Russian. There was a man either side of him and as he turned he saw three more close behind. 'What do you want?'

'Look there, please,' said one of them politely.

About a hundred and fifty yards along the concourse Hotovy saw his two boys being led into the building. There were three men and a woman with them. They went to the desk handling the Aeroflot flight. Tickets and boarding passes were handed to them without any checking formalities.

'You're not going to make a fuss, are you?' said the man.

'No,' said Hotovy.

It was two hours after the Aeroflot departure that Clarissa Willoughby arrived at Heathrow. With the porter trailing her she went straight by the check-in counter for the Nice flight to the ticket desk.

'I'd like to change my flight,' she said to the clerk.

The man in the grey suit, still with his umbrella, busied himself among the magazines at the bookstall. He found he read a lot in his line of business.

8

General Kalenin would have preferred more time to assemble the material but he was confident he had forgotten nothing. He arranged it before him on the desk top, checking against the carefully prepared list, for the final scrutiny. The medal ribbon designated a Hero of the Soviet Union and was accompanied by a long official citation made out in Charlie Muffin's name. There was a Soviet identity card, with a picture of Charlie and an authorization, again with a picture, for admission to the restricted concessionary stores. The passport contained Charlie's picture and was date-stamped for the relevant countries where the Britons had been killed. There was five thousand dollars in cash and several congratulatory cables, two referring to the assassinations in Delhi and Ankara. The longest document was the briefing about Rome. It ran to two full pages and Kalenin concentrated upon that most of all, because it had to complete the entrapment.

He summoned the courier to take it to the Foreign Ministry for inclusion in that night's diplomatic pouch to London, shrugging into his topcoat while he waited. He followed the messenger from his office but descended in the private lift directly into the basement where the car was waiting in an area of guaranteed absolute security. The journey to Kutuzovsky Prospect took only minutes and Kalenin dismissed the driver for the evening.

It was one of the largest apartments in the government complex, too big for his solitary needs but awarded to him because of his rank. The size enabled Kalenin to devote an entire room to his hobby. From habit he went immediately to it, staring down at the contoured papier-mâché layout and the positions of the miniature tanks with which he had been recreating the Battle of Kursk in the most recent war game. It was over a fortnight since he'd abandoned it. Normally he would have invited Alexei Berenkov to complete it with him, but had decided against it tonight.

Reminded of his guest, Kalenin went back into the main room and opened two bottles of Aloxe Corton to let them breathe. Berenkov preferred French to Russian wine and Kalenin enjoyed using his official position to indulge his friend. He lit a low heat beneath the bortsch and added meat and dumplings when it began to steam. He had just completed laying out the caviar and smoked fish when the bell sounded.

Berenkov entered as exuberantly as always, enveloping Kalenin in his burly arms. The only legacy of the man's British imprisonment was the white hair. The cowed apprehension of his immediate return had disappeared and under Valentina's care all the weight had been restored. He looked like a bear, thought Kalenin. But elderly and docile, the sort that live in children's fairy stories.

'Valentina is sorry,' said Berenkov, repeating the apology of their telephone conversation earlier in the day. 'I think Asian flu is the best weapon the Chinese have.'

'Tell her I hope she's better soon,' said Kalenin. 'But I wanted to talk to you alone anyway.'

For the caviar and fish there was vodka. Before they began eating they touched glasses, toasting Russian-fashion.

'That sounds intriguing,' said Berenkov, heaping his plate with fish.

'It's Charlie Muffin.'

Berenkov stopped eating, 'What about him?' There was a sadness of anticipation in his expression.

Berenkov had the highest security clearance for his appointment as senior lecturer at the spy college on the outskirts of Moscow, so Kalenin recounted in detail the Rome exposure and what he intended to do to save it. Berenkov sat hunched forward, huge hands cupped around his vodka glass, his food temporarily forgotten.

'He couldn't have been better for our purpose,' said Kalenin. Charlie Muffin had been responsible for trapping the other man and Kalenin knew that, during the debriefing which followed, a professional respect had developed between them.

'How did you find him?'

'In America, about a year ago,' said Kalenin. 'He was involved in the insurance protection of a Tsarist stamp collection. I've had him under observation ever since.'

'A convenient coincidence.'

'The British will be completely convinced.' Kalenin brought the bortsch and wine to the table. Berenkov poured, sniffing the bouquet appreciatively.

'What do you think of the plan?'

Berenkov made an uncertain rocking gesture with his hand. 'It seems good.'

'Kastanazy is being purged.' Kalenin needed to confide fully. 'I expect him to be dismissed any day.'

'Will you get the seat?'

Kalenin smiled. 'It's a possibility.'

Berenkov raised his glass. 'To your success.'

'Thank you.'

Berenkov put down the glass and said guardedly. 'You shouldn't underestimate Charlie Muffin.'

'He might have been good once,' agreed Kalenin. 'But not any longer: he's collapsed pretty badly during the last year.'

Berenkov laughed, a short, humourless sound. 'He was right about the stick,' he said.

'Stick?'

'A remark he made at the last meeting we had, in prison,' remembered Berenkov. 'He said he always got the shitty end of the stick.'

Charlie filled the bath with cold water, rolled up his trousers and perched carefully on the edge, easing his feet in with a sigh of relief. Rubber-soled suede wasn't good for hot weather: and now his feet hurt like buggery. He flexed his toes, thinking of the ride back to Rome.

Had there been a Lancia following? He'd only been aware

of it for part of the journey and when he'd slowed it had overtaken naturally enough. But he hadn't been going fast in the first place, so why had it crawled along behind?

Maybe he was being over-cautious. By going out to Ostia Charlie had avoided any contact with the embassy, so there couldn't be the slightest chance of detection. He would have to be careful he didn't imagine danger where none existed.

There was a knock at the door. It came again, more insistently, as he dried his feet. He padded across the room, without bothering to roll down his trousers.

'Going to the beach?' said Clarissa Willoughby.

'Just as soon as I knot my handkerchief,' said Charlie.

'You don't seem pleased to see me.'

'I'm not sure that I am.'

9

Clarissa sat in the middle of the bed with her knees drawn up beneath her chin, so that her skirt gaped, revealing too much leg. Charlie moved a crumpled shirt from the only chair in the room to sit down, wanting to distance himself from her. Charlie was annoyed. At Clarissa, for being so sure of herself. And at himself, for the excitement he felt.

'This is stupid,' he said.

'I don't think so.'

'I do.'

'It's fun.'

She meant it, Charlie knew. People like Clarissa did things simply because they were fun. Like boarding aircraft at dawn in the previous night's party clothes because breakfast at Focquets seemed fun, or like deciding it was fun to look at a friend's villa in Acapulco right after lunch at San Lorenzo. Clarissa must worry about her passport like he worried about his feet.

'What about Rupert?'

'He thinks I'm somewhere off the coast of Menton, on a yacht.'

'I didn't mean that.'

'Rupert didn't seem a problem for you in America. What's so different now?'

'Look at me,' said Charlie. 'I'm a worn-out old bugger at least ten years older than you. If you took me to the house of any of your friends they wouldn't let me past the kitchens.'

'You're an inverted snob!'

'Would they?'

'I don't intend finding out.' She looked around her. 'This is a pretty crappy room, Charlie.'

'I wasn't expecting to share it.'

'Are you going to?'

'I don't know.'

'Yes you do.'

'Isn't this a bit too much slam, bam, thank you, ma'am?'

'Being a prissy hypocrite doesn't suit you.'

'Flashing your arse doesn't suit you.'

A flush of anger picked out on her cheeks but she remained smiling. 'You thought it was a nice enough arse last time.'

This was how it had been in New York. He hadn't felt so emasculated by the approach then.

'We're the same,' Clarissa continued. 'Not quite, but almost. That's why it was so good. And will be again.'

He'd forgotten the disarming way she looked at anyone she was talking to, with those unnaturally pale eyes. He wanted her like hell. And she knew it.

'Go away Clarissa,' he said weakly.

'I've had a long journey,' she said. 'I'm tired and I want to go to bed.'

'They've probably got rooms.'

'I'm in one.'

'Stop it Clarissa!'

'Do you want me to?'

'Yes.'

'I don't believe you.'

'This is like.... ' Charlie waved his hands, as if he were trying to feel for the expression. ' ... it isn't real.'

'It's real enough for me.'

'Perhaps I haven't had the practice.'

'You're being a bore. You were never that, Charlie.'

'I was never raped, either.'

'I was once: it was fun.'

'Jesus!' said Charlie.

'I never knew his name. He was a chauffeur, in Spain. Being raped is a common female fantasy, you know?'

Clarissa rolled off the bed on the opposite side from him and said, 'Help me with the covers, Charlie.'

He hesitated. Then he got up from the chair and pulled them back on his side. She came over to him. 'And now unzip me.'

When the dress parted he saw she was not wearing a bra. She faced him as the dress fell to her feet and her hard-nippled breasts pushed up for attention. She reached for him and pulled his face to her. 'You didn't kiss me when I came in,' she said.

He did now, biting at her and she came back at him, just as anxiously. She brought her head back, panting and said, 'See! Just the same.'

'You make it seem as if you're trying to prove something.'

'Come to bed and prove something to me,' she said.

For Charlie it had been a long time and he was nervous, so he finished too quickly. She let him rest, holding him against her breast and gently stroking his head. Then she pushed him down and said, 'Now do it properly.'

He coaxed her gently, with his hands and mouth, holding back until she was almost ready before pushing into her. She strained up to meet him, head taut back for the groan that went on and on. When she spoke, the words quivered. '*That* was properly,' she said.

He turned onto his side, but didn't part from her and she held him tightly, to make sure he didn't.

'No point in all that posturing, was there?' she said.

'No.'

'Guilty?'

'Yes.'

'Sorry?'

'No.'

'Neither am I,' she said. 'But then I knew I wouldn't be.'

'What about all those animals you were supposed to be looking after?'

'I've found a hobby I like better,' she said.

Sir Alistair Wilson stood before the easels, comparing the photographs of Henry Walsingham and Richard Seming-ford. Ordinary, unremarkable people, he thought. But spies and traitors always looked like ordinary people, with mortgages and bills and kids at school and cars that went wrong.

The director turned at Harkness's entry.

'The replies are in,' announced the deputy, before he sat down. 'Thrown up a couple of things about Semingford.'

'What?'

'He's overdrawn, by about five hundred pounds. And there's an affair.'

'Don't these damned people ever think of blackmail before they take their trousers down?' said Wilson. 'Who is she?'

'Lady Billington's secretary, a girl named Jane Williams.'

'Background?'

'Admiral's daughter, from Devonport. Unmarried. Excellent grades in her civil service examinations.'

'How old?'

'Thirty.'

'How old is Semingford?'

'Forty-two.'

'The middle-aged wish to be young again: that's familiar too,' said the director. 'What about the security man?'

'Walsingham's financial affairs seem okay.'

'And the Australian inquiry?'

'Jill Walsingham's mother had a hysterectomy,' reported Harkness. As an afterthought, he added, 'It appears to have been successful.'

'Semingford's the most likely then?'

'I've told the people in Rome to concentrate upon him,' said Harkness. 'But it's not much, is it?'

The other man's caution was justified, conceded Wilson. 'Not really,' he agreed.

'Going to tell Naire-Hamilton?'

'No,' said Wilson. 'I'll wait until there's something firmer.' He looked back at the photographs. 'It's taking longer than I expected.'

'It's only been three days.' Harkness was surprised at the remark. 'And this is how it's got to be done, if they want discretion.'

'I know,' said Wilson. 'I'd just like a more positive development.'

'There is one.'

72

Wilson looked up.

'Hotovy didn't make his contact point. There were back-up rendezvous spots, for succeeding days. He hasn't shown at any of them.'

'What have you done?'

'Put the Czech embassy and all the residences under observation, since dawn. He's not been seen. Or the kids.'

'What about the wife?'

'Still no sign that she's returned from Brno.'

'He's gone then.'

'He was genuine,' said Harkness.

'If he'd crossed at once, he'd have been all right.'

'It would have been a hell of a coup, to have got him.'

'So it will be to get the bastard in Rome,' said Wilson.

10

Igor Solomatin arrived early at Doney's, wanting a pavement table from which he could see in both directions along the Via Veneto: he had people placed to guarantee that the Italian arrived alone, but still wanted personally to be sure. The evening promenade swirled back and forth in front of him. A parade of peacocks, thought the Russian. It wasn't criticism. The reverse, in fact. Solomatin knew he'd miss it. He'd miss the svelte, fur-coated women who always seemed to favour beige, and immaculate men whose shoes were always polished and who didn't look effeminate carrying wrist bags. And being able to sit outside cafés like now, and have waiters appear content to serve him instead of enduring the belligerent truculence of the steam-filled caverns of Moscow. And the clothes. Solomatin did not have the bulky Russian heaviness: he'd been chosen for the posting because the slightness, black hair and black eyes fitted easily into the Latin surroundings. Reverting to the square-shouldered, trouser-flapping creations of Moscow would be one of the small regrets he'd have. But very small. The Russian capital was where the promotion was: and Solomatin knew his promotion was inevitable after what was going to happen here. He'd been extremely fortunate.

Solomatin monitored the approach and checked the safety signals of his ground men before waving to the Italian whom he had cultivated for the past six months. Emilio Fantani was no longer the male prostitute he had been when he first arrived in Rome, but he still swayed between the tables with hip-swivelling suggestiveness. Solomatin noticed the eyes of several interested men as well as hopeful women follow the movement. Although he admired them, the clothes were too gaudy for Solomatin, silk floral shirt, black trousers and chamois jacket so thin as to be almost transparent, slung casually across the Italian's shoulders. Fantani had a jangle of gold bracelets on either wrist, in addition to the Cartier watch, and there was gold, too, circling his throat. He was a thin, wiry man, never appearing properly relaxed, with eyes that flickered constantly. Solomatin had never decided if he were seeking danger or prey.

When he reached the table, Fantani seemed out of breath, which Solomatin knew to be an affectation. 'I've kept you. Forgive me,' he said.

'I was early.' Solomatin always spoke carefully when addressing Fantani, not because of any problem with his vocabulary, which was excellent, but because of his accent. Fantani had been born in a peasant hut in Calabria, one of the poorest regions in Italy, but had lived off his wits in Rome since he was fourteen. He had a street-wise intelligence that was often disconcerting. Shortly after they met, Fantani had suddenly questioned Solomatin's pronunciation and queried outright whether he was Italian. Solomatin had talked of his birth in Tarvisio, on the Austrian border and of being brought up bi-lingually. Fantani appeared to accept it but at the time it frightened the Russian.

They shook hands and Fantani said, 'I was pleased to get your call.'

With every reason, thought Solomatin. It had been a careful softening-up period to convince Fantani he was being considered for graduation from cat burglar to organized crime. They had provided the man with four perfect robberies, with alarm systems and house plans and safe combinations that had taken the KGB squad months to assemble.

'It's big,' said Solomatin. 'I wanted to get everything right.'

A waiter came over and Fantani quickly ordered an Americano, impatient with the interruption.

'What is it?' he said.

'Jewellery.'

'Where?'

'The British ambassador has a villa at Ostia. It's in the safe there.'

Fantani's face creased. 'That's not just a robbery,' he said. 'That's political.'

More than you think, thought Solomatin. He said, 'You're not scared?'

'The security will be strong.'

'I've got all the details.'

'It'll be difficult to fence.'

'It'll be impossible,' said Solomatin. 'More than half is antique. It would be identified at once.'

Fantani stopped with the drink halfway to his lips. 'What's the point of stealing what we can't get rid of?'

'We're going to sell it back.'

'To the ambassador?'

Solomatin patiently shook his head. 'To the insurers. It's a common practice. The police don't like it, but the insurers do. It's cheaper to pay out a percentage than the full amount.'

'We'll do it together?'

'I'll tell you everything you have to do.' Solomatin had been maintaining a note of the time and was ready when Vasily Leonov edged onto a table three places away. It was unnecessary but Leonov had insisted upon using the meeting to identify his victim. The assassin showed no recognition. Within minutes of being seated, his concentration was entirely upon Fantani. Solomatin was too highly trained to show any outward reaction, but he felt an inner clutch of coldness: it was like watching a snake manoeuvre itself to strike at some tethered, helpless animal.

'How much information have you got?' said Fantani.

'Everything. Perimeter protection, alarm systems, safe location. The lot.'

'It sounds good.'

'It is.'

'When do I see it?'

Leonov had said he only wanted a few moments. 'Now,' said Solomatin.

Fantani's apartment overlooked the Piazza del Popolo, a

garish, harsh place of over-bright lighting, steel-framed furniture, see-through glass tables and black and white decor – an amalgam of a dozen film sets. Curtains were opened and closed from a central, electrically controlled panel, which also operated a television and stereo installation positioned like neat birds' nests in a lattice of tubular metal. It was the first time Solomatin had been there and Fantani was anxious to impress.

'A drink ... ?' He hesitated, gesturing towards a stone jar full of thickly rolled cigarettes. ' ... or something else?'

'Whisky,' said Solomatin. If he got the promotion he expected on his return to Moscow, he'd be able to buy Scotch at the concessionary stores: like the clothes, it was something he had come to enjoy.

Solomatin carried with him a slim document case. From it he took the information he had promised in the café, setting it out on one of the glass-topped tables.

'This is the big one, Emilio.'

'I've been waiting a long time.'

'It's got to work.'

'It will.' The assurance was too quick, too eager to please.

'Let's go through it.'

It took a long time, because Solomatin was aware his future was dependent upon it and was therefore determined there would not be any misunderstanding. He made the Italian study the perimeter protection, recite it back to him to guarantee it was memorized, and then study the plan of the villa and draw it himself, so that he would know the location of every room. Having established the design in Fantani's mind, the Russian insisted he itemize the entry points and mark upon his drawing the burglar protection. The final test was to recite the combination of the safe. It was fifteen minutes before Fantani got the numbering and dial changes correct; he was sweating and most of the bombastic composure was gone. Solomatin gathered up his own copies and returned them to the document case; if anything went wrong – which he was sure it couldn't – the only evidence would be in the Italian's own handwriting.

'It won't be easy,' Fantani was under no delusions. 'But there's a lot here. When do you want me to do it?'

'Tomorrow night.'

There was an almost imperceptible intake of breath. Then Fantani grinned in agreement. Solomatin remembered the way Leonov had looked at the man in the café and felt a sudden surge of pity. It was brief but it annoyed him; there wasn't any place for stupidity like that.

It was past midnight before Solomatin returned to his own apartment on the Via Mecanate. He put on the lights in a prepared sequence and sat down to wait. Leonov arrived after thirty minutes.

'Tomorrow night?' asked Leonov.

'Yes.'

'Sure he can do it?'

'We've tested him on four other burglaries; he's good.'

'He's flashy,' said Leonov. 'Is he homosexual?'

'Does it matter?'

'Don't like homosexuals,' said Leonov.

From their protracted observation, the Russians knew Charlie Muffin lived alone and there was no danger of sudden discovery. Nevertheless they were careful breaking into the Battersea flat, positioning lookouts in the corridor as well as the entrance to the block. Three men actually entered the apartment. Together with material that had been sent from Moscow, they carried an extensive range of workmen's tools; one had a small, battery-operated vacuum cleaner, to take the mess away with them afterwards. When they left, they removed the listening device that had been implanted in the telephone.

11

The table in the dressing room was set with a damask cloth and laid with glasses, ice bucket, bottles and water jug. It was within reaching distance of the chaise longue upon which Lady Billington lay, goblet in hand. 'Pell and Mell didn't like it,' she said.

'What?' said Charlie.

'The cats. They spend all their time with me. They're locked up with Jane and they don't like it.'

Charlie didn't imagine that Jane Williams would like it much either. He carried his drink to the bureau. He knelt before it, released the securing bolt and eased sideways the left-hand pedestal leg. The face of the floor-mounted safe was about two feet in diameter, the combination dial snug in the centre.

'Hector used to suffer from allergies,' said Lady Billington. 'Took a course of injections for it once.'

'I tried,' said Charlie. 'It didn't work. Have I your permission to open the safe?'

'Do you need it?'

'It seems so.'

'Go ahead.'

Charlie huddled over the insurance guide to the safe combination, turning the numerals into position. At the final click he didn't lift the lid at once, but felt carefully beneath. 'There isn't a breaker alarm,' he said.

Lady Billington was leaning forwards towards the table. 'Should there be?'

'It's not listed,' admitted Charlie. 'But I would have expected one.'

'Better ask Hector,' she said. 'How's your drink?'

'Fine, thank you.'

Charlie lifted the covering upon a miniature cavern carved out below. The cleverness of the concealment denied the normal facilities of shelves and the boxes were stacked one on top of the other. Charlie lifted them out, first to the mouth of the safe and then across the room to arrange before Lady Billington. Automatically he separated the newer-looking containers from the old. Seeing the division she said, 'There's a lot of heirlooms.'

'I've read the policy,' said Charlie.

'Don't wear the old stuff much,' she confessed. 'Most of it is too big. I feel like a shire horse decorated for the country fair.'

'It's an awful lot of brass,' said Charlie, flattening the noun for the north-country meaning. She laughed.

It was a dazzling kaleidoscope of wealth, the red of rubies and iced white of diamonds, the dull white of pearls and the greens and blues of emeralds and sapphires. Briefly he was reminded of the bridge lights over the Thames on those stumbling nights towards Battersea.

'Better have a drink before we start,' suggested Lady Billington.

'Why not?' said Charlie. It didn't seem he was alone in drinking when he was bored. Her appearance wasn't affected yet; perhaps it had only just started.

'Will I have to do this every year?' The hiss was more obvious when she spoke.

'Probably,' said Charlie.

'How do you want to do it?'

'As it comes, I suppose.'

'Cheers,' she said.

'Cheers.'

Charlie might once have argued it impossible for it to be tedious physically to handle one and a half million pounds' worth of jewellery, but it was. He had to locate on his list whatever Lady Billington produced to compare with the accompanying photograph and description, check the setting and stone content and then restore it to the safe to avoid confusion with what remained. Quickly all awareness of what he was touching disappeared. Cosmetic surgeons doing breast operations probably felt the same way.

Lady Billington treated the business with the same casual detachment. After an hour she said, 'When Hector said this was legally necessary I thought it was a good idea. Now I'm not so sure.'

'It's best to be careful,' said Charlie. She stretched her legs out along the chaise longue, so he eased himself onto the dressing-table stool, flexing the cramp from his legs. Pieces of fluff from the carpet speckled his trousers.

'Quite frankly I couldn't give a damn,' she said. 'Surprised?'

'Yes,' said Charlie.

'Right that you should be,' she said. 'Just as I should be surprised at the poor little rich girl feeling.'

The confessional of gin, thought Charlie. It was tenuous but Charlie decided there was a similarity between this woman and the one he had left in bed at the hotel. Lady Billington sought her escape in a bottle and Clarissa in bed. He felt a twitch of anger towards both of them.

Lady Billington stirred a box with her feet; a rope of pearls, Charlie knew.

'Know what I think sometimes when I'm putting these things on?'

'What?'

'How many empty bellies they could fill.'

She was draining bottles and putting messages inside, he thought. 'Why don't you give them away then? Save this sort of thing every year.'

She smiled wearily. 'All the old stuff is in family trust anyway,' she said. 'And there is already a charity established: something to do with bringing Africans to England to train them to be agronomists. My father set it up.'

'Aren't there organizations you could become involved with?'

'International committees flying first class to New York or Geneva and eating six-course banquets and agreeing how beastly it is for people to starve.'

He'd been wrong about Lady Billington. She was a woman brim full of sadness. 'It's an uneven world,' agreed Charlie.

'That's trite,' she said.

'But true.'

Lady Billington added unsteadily to her glass, spilling some onto the cloth so that a damp grey stain spread across it. '"From each according to his abilities ... to each according to his needs,"' she quoted indistinctly.

'Is that the Karl Marx original or the *Oxford Book of Quotations*?'

'Political science. Girton. A poor Second.'

Charlie indicated the boxes and then spread his hands to include the villa. 'Do you need all this?'

'Truth is I'm not sure,' she admitted. 'Couldn't give a damn about the jewellery. But I don't think I want to get rid of everything. ... ' She smiled wearily again. 'Am I making sense?'

'Vaguely.'

'I shouldn't drink so much.'

'It's an easy habit to get into,' said Charlie with feeling. 'Shouldn't we get on?'

'How's your drink?'

'All right, thank you.'

'Don't suppose I should,' she said reluctantly.

It took a further hour to complete the jewellery inventory. They finished with Lady Billington's engagement ring, which was the only piece she hadn't returned to the safe in preparation for his visit.

'One for the road,' she insisted.

'A small one.'

She looked at him curiously. 'You've got bits all over your clothes.'

Charlie made an ineffective attempt to sweep away the carpet debris. Lady Billington gazed vaguely around the dressing room. 'Suppose there should be a brush somewhere.'

'Don't bother.'

'Do you need to see my husband for anything?' she said.

'If you do, it'll have to be at the embassy.'

Charlie shook his head in instant rejection. 'No,' he said. The whole business had been remarkably straightforward. How easy would it be to persuade Willoughby to employ him more regularly? The idea settled and he decided it was a good one: anything was better than the state into which he had been crumbling. Charlie's mind blocked at the thought. What about Clarissa?

They left through the ambassador's bedroom and Lady Billington stopped near the oar-blade display. 'Have you seen these?' she said, the pride obvious.

Charlie went alongside her. Lady Billington's finger traced a line along the photographs of her husband in the university rowing team. 'He was almost chosen for the Olympics,' she said.

Although he'd looked at them before, Charlie politely studied the pictures again. All assured, confident, good-looking young men, their places in life guaranteed by name and influence. Lucky buggers.

They left the bedroom and Lady Billington walked with him down the marbled staircase and along the corridor to the door. 'Forgive the maudlin,' she said.

'Thanks for the drink.'

'Drive carefully.'

'Don't worry.'

Charlie was an intuitive man, reacting to feelings and to impressions. And the feeling at the moment was uncertainty. As he took the hire car down the tree-lined driveway he tried to find a reason for it. He'd avoided absolutely any contact with the embassy and the security check had been what he had anticipated in Willoughby's office, a job for a clerk. So why the unease? On the return to Rome Charlie maintained a regular speed and constantly checked his rear-view mirror; today there was no obvious pursuit. He must have imagined the blue Lancia, like everything else. It had to be Clarissa.

She was already in the hotel room when he got there, surrounded by packages and parcels, like a child who'd found its way into Santa's storeroom.

'I've had a *fantastic* time,' she said. 'My American Express card is like a piece of rubber.'

'I felt like that this morning,' said Charlie.

'I can fix that.'

'Won't Rupert wonder at purchases in Rome when you're supposed to be off the coast of France on a yacht?'

'Oh, bugger Rupert,' she said carelessly. 'He never notices anything anyway.'

In the foyer downstairs, a patient man in a grey suit carefully folded the newspaper he couldn't read because it was in Italian, and made another precise entry in a notebook. Already the list was extensive.

Henry Jackson was a large, soft-fleshed man who would have looked the part astride a policeman's bicycle on an English country beat. It was an impression he purposely conveyed because it made people careless. He was, in fact, extremely astute and even, when the occasion demanded, physically quick, which was why Harkness had chosen him to supervise the British field team in Rome. Henry Walsingham greeted him with the withdrawn friendliness of an out-of-town representative undergoing an annual visit from head office. Jackson emphasized plodding officialdom. He insisted upon a complete tour of every department, hoping to gauge the required degree of efficiency from the behaviour of the staff and the material on their desks. In one office overlooking the Via Settembre he identified Richard Semingford. The Second Secretary looked up in mild interest at the intrusion and then returned to his work. There were marines on guard in the cipher and vault room and every check and identification was observed. Jackson remained for some time in the cipher room, stressing its importance for the forthcoming Summit for direct communication between the Premier and his ministers in Italy with the cabinet in London. It would be necessary for him to instal someone over a longer period, but Jackson's initial impression was that the security was being maintained at the proper level. Back in Walsingham's office, he allowed himself to be taken through the list of every official and unofficial function in which the British party would be involved. Indexed against each function were details of the security provisions made by the Italian government.

'There's extensive use of helicopters.'

'So I see.'

'The whole thing is an obvious target for the Red Brigade,' said the embassy security man. Even when he was supposedly relaxed there was a military uprightness about him.

'That's our assessment as well.'

'The Italians are worried.'

'With every reason to be.'

'Still didn't expect a visit from you people quite so soon,' said Walsingham. 'There's a lot of time left.'

'Better to be safe than sorry,' said Jackson. It was the sort of remark the other man would expect. 'I've brought five people with me. I want to move them into the embassy tomorrow.'

'What for?'

'Familiarize themselves with the working of the place,' said Jackson. 'Find out where the lavatories and the different departments are.'

'I think I should advise the ambassador.' Walsingham was a man who always deferred to a superior officer.

'Of course.'

'What *exactly* will they be doing?'

'Poking around the cipher room and vaults mostly.'

'Why?'

'I've told you,' said Jackson patiently. 'It's from there all the stuff will be going back to London. Don't want any embarrassments, do we?'

Indignation showed upon Walsingham's face. 'There is nothing wrong with the security at this embassy,' he said stiffly.

'I'm sure there's not,' said Jackson, at once placatory. He spread his hands, entering the charade he was sure the other man would accept, 'Not my decision, old boy. You know what it's like at Whitehall: they still use initials instead of proper names for the director and talk about moles and daft stuff like that.'

85

There was a complete surveillance operation upon Henry Walsingham and Richard Semingford when they left the embassy that evening. Walsingham went to his apartment overlooking the Tiber and remained there. Semingford met Jane Williams at a café on the Via Condotti. They had a drink, walked a short distance to a restaurant where they ate early, and went back to her apartment. Semingford was still there at midnight and all the lights were out.

'Why the hell didn't one of the bastards react!' demanded Jackson irritably, when the reports were brought back to him at the Eden. 'I was supposed to have made one of them nervous.'

Kalenin used the best calligraphist but, even so, limited the entries to initialled notations in Charlie Muffin's name and to the signatures against the bank authority. There were four genuine messages of top-secret classification which he had received from the British embassy in Rome re-copied on paper brought in from Italy to satisfy any forensic test. The reference to the earlier meeting with Charlie Muffin in Washington the previous June was provably upon Russian foolscap and he hesitated, looking down at it. They had identified Charlie in Florida on 15 June, but, from the checks later, Kalenin knew the stamp exhibition had been in New York from 8 June. From New York it was easier to reach Washington than from Palm Beach, just an hour on the shuttle. It was the sort of detail that was important; 10 June was perfect. He put it with the other documents, then another Russian foolscap containing all the information about the combination and security precautions at Billington's Ostia villa. The final, fittingly cosmetic, touch was ten thousand dollars in American currency.

Kalenin had just addressed it for diplomatic transport to Igor Solomatin in Rome when the message arrived from London about the previous shipment. The hidden compartment had been fixed below the base of a bedroom closet and all the material placed in it. They were confident it would be found, but only after a rummage search.

Kalenin sat back at his desk, allowing himself a brief

moment of satisfaction. Almost immediately he rose to his feet. Alexander Hotovy had undergone sufficient preparation. Everything was going too well to allow uncertainty, and Kalenin was anxious to satisfy himself the Czech did not represent any greater danger than he already imagined.

12

Emilio Fantani had a criminal's ability to distinguish between true wealth and surface glitter, and as he rounded the promontory on the Ostia road to gaze down upon the Billington villa he knew this was true wealth. Unlike Charlie Muffin, who had taken the same route earlier, Fantani slowed and then stopped, using the elevation of the hill for his reconnaissance. The angle prevented his establishing a seafront approach, but there would obviously be one leading up to the grape and flower hung verandah he could just determine at the right-hand side of the house.

With a burglar's patience he waited for thirty minutes slumped back in his seat, ensuring the information about no ground patrol was correct before releasing the handbrake to coast down under minimal power towards the entrance. He was briefly aware of the men in the gate lodge but his concentration was upon the electrical wiring thatched along the top of the walls.

The sea, he decided, reverting to his original intention. There was a layby almost at the junction of the Pratica road and as he reached it Fantani saw the parked police car. It was unmarked but identifiable from the heavy radio antennae that was always mounted in the roof; as discreet as elephants in ballet slippers, he thought. There were three men inside the yellow vehicle, lounged back with the practice of those who spend a lot of time waiting for things to happen.

Fantani didn't slow. To his right the sun sparked off the polished water and far out to sea a clutch of fishing boats moved sedately along the skyline, like ducks in a line. The hills were ochre and bald, patched occasionally with thin grass. Hobbled goats, neck bells jangling, nuzzled hopefully and once Fantani had to brake and swerve to avoid one that started into the road to tug at a suddenly discovered tuft.

It took longer than Fantani wanted before he found a cliff break to get down to the beach. He parked and took a towel and the raffia mat from the rear seat. Descending the looped pathway, he set out through the foot-sucking sand and shingle in the direction of the villa. It took an hour and Fantani was glad he had allowed himself so much time. He stopped some way from the barrier that made the ambassador's beach private. Fantani had come prepared, already wearing a costume beneath his clothes. He spread the mat, undressed and folded everything neatly before stretching out, apparently to sunbathe. For almost half an hour he did, before turning over onto his stomach to begin the examination. The beach fence was high and spike-topped and projected some unseen distance into the water. Fantani did not think it was insurmountable. It didn't matter anyway, he decided, looking to the cliff face. It might have been possible to scale once, but from the artificially smooth surface of the rocks he guessed it had been blasted away to create the almost perpendicular drop.

Like a black line drawn down it, there was a smoked-glass lift linking the villa to the sea, and alongside the zigzag of emergency steps. It would only need one man at the top to protect both approaches. Fantani squinted up against the sun at the villa, locating more pillars and bourgainvillea. It was at the point where the protective estate wall abutted the cliff that Fantani stopped. The wall had been brought to the edge and from the conduit box which stuck up like a proud thumb he guessed the electrical connection stopped there. The screen was completed by a wide half-circle of meshed spikes, splayed out like a woman's fan against the wall end and the cliff face, over a drop which Fantani estimated at four hundred metres but accepted would probably be more, because of his shortened elevation. He smiled, seeing the way, and turned over onto his back again to doze in the sun. For another hour he relaxed, then dressed and rolled up his mat, leaving his shoes and socks off for the gritty walk back to the car.

It was still only four in the afternoon so Fantani continued towards Pratica until he found the first roadside café. He considered a brandy but decided his nerves didn't need any help. Instead he took coffee.

Life was good, decided Fantani. And going to get better. A lot better. It had taken long enough; nearly fifteen years of screwing and being screwed, trinket stealing from those who wouldn't risk complaint, and then the gradual reputation as a competent craftsman. He knew it was the reputation that had prompted the approach. Only two arrests and both unimportant. It was the sort of thing the big organizers liked: style and expertise. Fantani had no doubt whom he was working for; who else but the Mafia had the organization to get the details he'd been provided with? It had been a trial period; with this the final test. When he passed he'd learn who the man was. Fantani was sure the name wasn't Jacono. But he'd never shown any curiosity or tried to question. They respected attitudes like that. Style, thought Fantani again.

Driving back towards Ostia, Fantani saw that, because of a kink in the coastline, the sun was setting on the landward, not the seaward, side, which was an advantage: already, to his left, the darkness was merging the clifftop blackly with the water. Fantani took the Fiat up a track, so that it would be completely concealed from the road, and stood against the open boot, changing into the clothing in which he worked. Everything was black for concealment, even the canvas shoes. Before putting on the sweater, he taped to one wrist the electrical bypass leads and to the other the glass-cutter. He kept the trouser pockets free for ease of movement but carefully zipped inside the cotton windcheater the collapsible silk bag, the plans of the villa and its burglar protection, the doctor's stethoscope with a shortened length of tubing, and the tape roll. Satisfied with his preparations, he completed the last part of the ritual, relieving himself against the wheel of the car.

He positioned himself carefully during the final approach

to the villa neither too near the road, where he would be visible to passing vehicles, nor too near the cliff edge, where he might be seen against the slightly lighter skyline. Three times cars swept along the coast road but on each occasion their lights warned him long before their arrival and he was crouched low and completely hidden when they passed.

He was adjusted to the darkness when he got to the villa perimeter, conscious of the solid blackness of the wall. Near to it, Fantani squatted, settling himself for the wait, head tensed to one side for any animal or human sound to indicate a regular patrol he'd failed to detect from the overlooking hill. It was thirty minutes before he moved, sure there was none.

Near the clifftop the wind was stronger, blowing harder against him than he had expected. He hoped it wouldn't cause difficulties. Where the wall ended he crouched again, gazing out at the fan-like half-circle, wanting to impress everything about it into his mind. There were about forty spikes, spear-shaped at their ends and patterned together by looped metal spokes radiating outwards; closer, Fantani saw it exactly like a spider's web cut in half. He groped about his feet, discarding the first two things his hand encountered and finally locating a stick stout enough for the purpose. He edged closer, so he wouldn't be defeated by the wind, and threw it at the metal, eyes half closed for a spark of contact if the electrification had been continued in some way he hadn't identified. The twig hit the metal, without any flash, lodged for a few moments between one of the supporting arms and fell away into the darkness below. Fantani was able to trace its descent, because floodlights had been switched on from the villa. By leaning out slightly he could look down at the ambassador's private beach. At the foot of the cliff a jetty nosed out into the black water and a speedboat jostled at a mooring.

Fantani spread his hands along his thighs, massaging them in readiness for the jump, taking in deep breaths to calm himself. The wind was gusting and he stayed crouched, waiting for it to drop. He started to go and faltered, settling down again, angry at the hesitation. He squeezed the tension out of his hands, coiled ready, and when the wind lessened launched himself outwards. He leaped spreadeagled, arms and legs wide for any support, aiming for the widest part of the half-circle. The villa floodlighting helped, silhouetting the outline as he arced towards it, over the four-hundred metre drop.

Fantani landed well, both hands connecting with one of the horizontal bars and his left foot slotting into place. He winced as his unsupported right shin hit the metal before he got a foothold there. He was completely exposed now, like some insect trapped in the spider's web of metal, the wind plucking at his clothing and strong enough to sting his eyes. He hung there, recovering his composure, and then crabbed out further, towards the speared ends. Near the edge he paused, preparing himself for the strain. He propped his right arm inside the furthermost spoke and wedged his foot. For several seconds he hung, with his left arm and leg dangling free and unsupported, then he grabbed around the points, snatching for purchase on the other side. The tips pressed against the entire length of his body as if he were being impaled, and he winced against the pressure; they were sharper than he had expected them to be. First his hand and then his leg connected. He gripped tightly, anchoring his body, then released his right hand and pulled himself in a swinging manoeuvre around the barrier to gain the villa side.

Fantani had to climb up the web to bring himself level with the cliff and feel with his foot, without being able to look backwards, for solid ground. With a toehold, he levered himself further onto the cliff. Fantani was stretched out now, feet on the cliff and hands clinging to the metal struts, his back bent painfully between. Using the strength from his shoulders, Fantani heaved himself up onto the cliff, until there was solid ground to the level of his chest and he could release the metal without overbalancing onto the beach below.

Fantani was panting and wet with sweat, which was drying coldly against his face and back. He was shaking and knew the coldness was only partially responsible. They'd made the final acceptance job bloody difficult.

At last he stood, vaulted the fence, and pulled into the protection of some trees; cypresses, just like the driveway. They had been planted in a regimented line, close-patterned, and the permanent shadows made perfect cover. It took him almost to the house, sufficiently close to gaze in through the uncurtained windows. It was a kitchen area, with the servants' quarters alongside. At first he thought there were eight around the table but then a girl appeared, waiting upon the others. So the ambassador and his wife must be at the residence in Rome; that was going to make it easier.

He retreated from the lighted part of the house, still using the tree concealment to gain the darkened wall. He hunched, trying to recall from the plans inside his jacket where he was. The identified kitchen provided the guide. West wing, nearest the drive; that meant the study and drawing rooms. There were breaker points on the window sashes and verandah windows to the study, according to the plans. Fantani moved forward, confirming the layout when he got nearer. He went confidently to the drawing room window, counting first laterally and then horizontally the paned windows, isolating the third from the ground. He unstrapped the glass-cutter from his wrist and incisively arced an area. He gummed tape strips across the cut line, to prevent the glass either shattering or falling noisily into the room, and cuffed it with the heel of his hand. It broke cleanly, swinging inwards on the sticky tape hinges. Fantani eased in his hand, feeling for the connections between the doors which, if broken, would sound the alarm. They jutted out like nipples and Fantani fingered them familiarly. He took the bypass leads from his other wrist, shook out the wire to give him the maximum entry when the doors opened and went in again through the hole, attaching the alligator clips to each nipple. Fantini counted up again to get alongside the latch, and made another entry like the first. He'd been prepared for the lock to be empty, but the key was carelessly in place. He turned it, depressed the handle and, hesitating only momentarily, pushed the door open to the full extent of the bypass leads. There was no jangle of alarms.

Fantani, forewarned, did not walk directly in but short-

93

stepped sideways, avoiding the secondary alarm system activated by the pressure pads beneath the window carpeting.

Clear of the French windows, he went cautiously towards the door leading further into the house, hands held out for any obstruction. At the door he stopped, listening with his head close against a panel. From the other side there was silence. Cautious still, Fantani pushed open the door and waited again. There was no sound. He widened it sufficiently to see out and ensure the corridor was empty, emerging into the brightly lit passageway. He'd been in darkness for so long that the suddenness of the light burst at him. He blinked against it, anxious for darkness again. The approach to the second storey curved around the rim of the vestibule, a broad, sweeping staircase wide enough for at least four people to ascend, all comfortably abreast. Fantani ran up lightly, pausing at the top to regain his sense of direction. Guest bedrooms left and right, master suite ahead with the best view of the Tyrrhenian Sea. At the door he paused, listening again for any noise from inside. Although he heard nothing, Fantani was not satisfied. He gently lowered the handle and eased the door ajar, standing back to run if there was a sudden challenge. There was nothing. Fantani hurried in, securing the door behind him, alert for the deep breathing of someone asleep. He checked that the drapes were closed and actually felt out over the bed, as a final insurance against its being occupied, before he put on the light.

This wasn't a shared bedroom, Fantani knew at once. Only a man had ever slept here: a proud man, conscious of his success. Near the dressing table there was a bust, which Fantani presumed to be the ambassador. By switching on the light he'd activated the spotlight cleverly mounted alongside one of the wardrobes: it gave the carving a godlike appearance. The Italian's eyes moved uninterestedly over the pictures and diplomas, stopping at the bed. It was turned back only on one side, with pyjamas neatly laid out. So they weren't sleeping at the official residence.

Spurred by the warning, Fantani hurried to what was obviously the communicating door, looking for the room that

94

had been identified on the documents he'd studied. The dressing room was a large, square place lined with cupboards, apart from one entire wall elaborately arranged as a woman's make-up area, with lights fixed carefully around the mirror. Fantani took it all in at a glance, seeking the desk. He drew the safe blueprint from his jacket, laying it out beside him on the floor. There was no disturbance of the carpet to indicate how the pedestal might turn and Fantani felt a momentary lurch of uncertainty. He groped back, beneath the leg area. The securing bolt came snugly beneath his fingers. He slid it easily aside and pushed, lightly at first and then more strongly. The left support swivelled sideways. Fantani stooped low inside the cramped space, positioning the shortened stethoscope against the combination dial. He began to sweat again because of the nervousness and the tightly enclosed space, impatient for the numbers to co-ordinate with their code and snap into place. Around him the house remained quiet and undisturbed.

At the count of seven, Fantani began gently easing the lid: it lifted at nine. He stopped abruptly, taking the thin tip of the glass-cutter and running it gently beneath the rim, feeling for any alarm trigger. Satisfied there was none, Fantani lifted the top off completely, staring down inside the safe, feeling the sharp burst of sensual pleasure more intense than he ever felt gazing at the naked body of a waiting woman. Beneath the circular opening the safe opened into a square retaining area and in it jewel boxes and containers were stacked like bricks in a child's construction game.

Fantani took the cases individually from the safe, emptying their contents into the silk bag. Every colour in the spectrum dazzled up at him, reds and greens and blues and iced white, and he felt the excitement block in his throat. His hand was shaking when he replaced the safe top and twirled the dial to lock it. He re-positioned the covering pedestal and swept his hand across the carpet to erase any signs of disturbance. He decided to leave as he had entered, through the male bedroom. He turned off the dressing-room lights, crossed the darkened room and eased open the door to the landing and the widely sweeping staircase. He was halfway out when he heard the woman's voice, talking animatedly, before he snatched back into the bedroom.

He was trapped. .

The interrogation rooms were subterranean, far below ground level, but there was no dungeon impression. They were reached by a smooth operating lift and the corridors were rubber-tiled and well lighted by concealed strips behind unbreakable overhead glass, so that it appeared more like a hospital.

Hotovy was in one of the central rooms. Kalenin stopped just inside the door. The man was in a sitting position but not really in a chair. It was a metal frame, moulded to support a human shape. Hotovy was clamped into it, completely naked, with metal bands around his wrists, arms, waist, ankles and thighs, making him utterly immobile. There was also a band around his neck to keep him upright. The finger ends were pulped and crushed and electrodes were pasted to his genitals and nipples. Where he had been forced up against the tethering, in the agony of the current being applied, his body was purpled and bloodied. There were some haphazard whip marks across his chest and thighs, and his face was swollen and bruised. The eyes moved, although dully, at Kalenin's entry. There was a telephone just inside the door and Kalenin used it to summon the waiting doctors. There were three of them.

'What exactly do you want?' asked the physician in charge.

'Complete awareness,' said Kalenin. 'He's got to recognize others can suffer as he has.'

'For how long?'

Kalenin shrugged. 'A brief confession. There's only one thing I really want to know.'

'Any concern about lasting effects?'

'None.'

They set up an intravenous drip and then examined Hotovy for internal injuries. There was some spleen and liver enlargement, which they diagnosed as bruising, but an encephalogram disclosed no brain damage. Hotovy was already stirring when they prepared the other injections. The first stimulant they put into his arm, but the second, larger, dose they pumped directly into the aorta, an insertion only normally used for resuscitation after a heart collapse. Hotovy's recovery was dramatic and complete, to full consciousness. Kalenin had expected the man to show fear: certainly there was apprehension but there was still a sullen resistance.

'Thirty minutes,' estimated the chief surgeon.

'Bring him,' ordered Kalenin, striding from the room.

Supported by guards on either side Hotovy was hauled, feet dragging, behind the KGB chief. It was only a few yards to the other side of the interrogation area. Here the chambers were larger and partitioned, so that observers could watch questioning unseen from a soundproofed box. Behind the glass, Hotovy's wife and two sons sat cowed on a central bench. The woman wore a shapeless prison dress and the boys were clinging to her, terrified. As they watched, one gave way and began to cry and the woman pulled him into her shoulder to comfort him.

Hotovy gave a cut-off, strangled moan and pushed forward against the glass. The guards were ready and held him back. The Czech's head moved, like a boxer who has taken too much punishment. 'No,' he said. 'Please no.'

'Rome,' demanded Kalenin. 'What did you tell the British about Rome?'

Hotovy looked round bewildered. 'Rome?' he said. 'I told them nothing about Rome.'

It was a genuine confession, thought Kalenin. 'You made a query to your ministry in Prague. About British concern at our expansion in Africa. There's a file record.'

'Only for the designation of source,' whimpered Hotovy. 'And that was Cape Town: Rome was never mentioned.'

Kalenin went to the microphone linking him to the men standing over the woman and boys, on the other side of the screen. Hotovy moaned again when he saw the Russian reach out for the control switch.

'What about Rome?' persisted Kalenin.

'I don't know anything about Rome!' wailed Hotovy. 'On my life!'

'It's not your life,' said Kalenin, 'it's theirs.'

'I don't know *anything* about Rome. For God's sake, believe me!'

Kalenin did. Which meant the damage was no more extensive than he already knew it to be. Abruptly he turned on his heel and left the room.

The chief doctor caught up with him at the lift entrance. 'That was a massive stimulant,' said the man. 'I'd guess a collapse, almost at once. It'll be severe.'

Kalenin turned, as the doors opened. 'He's not important any more,' he said.

Richard Semingford was a precise, neat man, given to blazers with club buttons and ties, club-striped too. He had a close-clipped beard, and on the first night they had slept together in her apartment Jane Williams had produced a picture of her bearded father in naval uniform, and they'd tried to remember the opposite of an Oedipus complex and failed. They had made love there again tonight but not well and now they lay in the darkness, side by side but untouching.

'You didn't have to buy the meal,' he said.

'I know things aren't easy,' she said.

'It costs a lot, maintaining Ann's mother in that damned old people's home. And there are a lot of things the Foreign Office doesn't pay for, with the kids' schooling.'

'I said I don't mind,' she reminded him.

'I do.'

She felt out for his hand. 'You shouldn't. I love you and I understand.'

'I want to ask Ann for a divorce.'

'Is that sensible?'

'No.' He kissed her on the cheek. 'She might have relaxed her Catholic principles to marry a Protestant but I'm pretty sure she wouldn't about divorce.'

'So what's the point?'

'Permission isn't necessary any more.'

'She could still make it unpleasant: the Foreign Office doesn't like personal unpleasantness, you know.'

'She might not, if she thought she was being properly provided for.'

She squeezed his hand. 'And how could you do that, darling? You can't manage as it is.'

His hand tightened upon hers. 'That's the bloody problem,' he said. 'It's always money.'

She tried to think of something to break his mood and said, 'We had an awful man out at the villa.'

'Who?'

'Some insurance assessor, checking Lady Billington's jewellery. Frightful person.'

'What was wrong with him?'

'Cocksure, for a start. Literally. I could practically feel his hand up my skirt.'

'What's his name?'

'I never bothered to find out. I used to see men like him wandering the streets of Portsmouth and Chatham when daddy was on base, stumbling from pub to pub and leering at any girl they saw.' Once more, the morning's indignation was building up within her. 'Bloody cats made him sneeze and I had to look after the damned things.'

'What did Lady Billington think?'

'You know her. The social conscience of the world! She thinks everyone's wonderful.'

'Mustn't it be marvellous to have the Billingtons' money?' said Semingford. 'Never again having to bother about end-of-month sums on the backs of envelopes.'

'I've never thought about it.'

'Because you never had to.' He regretted it at once and said, 'I'm sorry.'

'It doesn't matter.'

'It does and I'm sorry: really I am. I'll get the money and divorce Ann.'

'Of course,' she said.

'Don't patronize me.'

'I didn't mean to.'

'But you did.'

'And you were rude.'

'I meant it, about divorcing Ann,' he said.

'Don't do anything silly, darling,' she said. 'I'm happy enough, the way things are.'

'I'm not,' he said grim-faced.

13

In his initial panic, Fantani ran halfway across the bedroom, which was a mistake. By the time he'd realized it, they were outside, so there was nothing he could do but make for the dressing room. He was caught like a rat in a trap! And with nowhere to hide. He couldn't risk any of the closets because they might be opened on him. The extravagantly lighted dressing table was built into the wall, with no gap for concealment. And there was no cover by the desk. He heard the outer door open and close in the adjoining room and the light drove a silver brightness beneath the door. Almost at once there was the sound of the far door to the woman's room and then the light snapped on.

There was only the window area. It was the part of the room he'd studied least of all, vaguely remembering an ornate couch and heavy drapes. He felt out, sliding his foot gently across the carpeting to avoid a noisy collision. He brushed lightly into the chaise longue, groping down for the arm and sweeping his hand cautiously before him, to ensure his path was clear. Suddenly he felt velvet between his fingers. He reached behind the curtains, every nerve end strained for a place beyond. There was a space! Groping blindly, his hands hit the sharp edge of the venetian blinds; they rattled slightly against the window and Fantani jerked back. His next move was more cautious, easing the curtains apart and then feeling forward to gauge the distance. A metre, no more: hardly a body width. And with the blinds at his back ready to clatter if he relaxed for a moment. Fantani pressed through, pulling himself sideways at the sound of footfalls. At once the room flooded with light and Fantani closed his eyes in despair. There was a parting between the curtain edges, where he'd failed to close them; the light shafted through against the window, providing him with a perfect reflection of the room. And if either one looked too closely into the extensive, brightly lit mirroring against the wall of the dressing room, they would see him.

It was a woman and she was naked, the evening gown crumpled in her hand. She tossed it onto the couch on her way to the dressing table. Not completely naked, he corrected; there were still the rings and the ruby choker and the matching earrings. She began leisurely to unfasten them, concentrating not upon what she was doing but upon her body. About forty-five, estimated Fantani with professional expertise. But she'd taken care. There was hardly any droop to her ass and she'd retained the muscle control of her stomach, so that there was no unsightly bulge when she relaxed. She tossed one earring onto the table in front of her and cupped a full breast in either hand, lifting them, so the nipples rose like the noses of inquiring puppies.

'Hector!' she called.

'What?' came a muffled voice.

'I'm sure that woman with the German ambassador has had her breasts lifted.'

'It was his wife.'

'What's that got to do with it?'

'Didn't think you knew who she was.'

'Of course I knew who she was. Do you think she has?'

'What?'

'Had her breasts lifted?'

'I didn't look.'

'With a dress like that it was hardly necessary. I wonder if it hurts?'

Fantani heard but didn't see the other door open into the room. 'How should I know?'

The man came into view; he was wearing a robe but his socks were still supported by old fashioned suspenders, secured in an elasticized band just beneath the knee.

'I sag,' complained the woman. 'Do you think I sag?'

'Let go.'

She lowered her hands and her breasts slumped.

'They're fine.'

'Sometimes dresses are better without a bra.'

'Middle-aged wives of ambassadors don't walk about with their nipples sticking out. And they don't stay so close to the cocktail waiter.'

She unfastened the other earring, then the necklace, and began creaming the make-up from her face. 'I've never let you down.'

'Not yet.'

'Frightened that I might?'

'I just wish you'd cut it down a little.'

Fantani's body began to ache with the effort of holding himself away from the blinds and his legs began to shake. Get out, he prayed, desperately; in the name of Jesus and Mary, get out!

'You're not worried about something, are you?' he said.

'Of course not.'

'I'd like you to be careful over the next few weeks,' said Billington. 'We're going to be under the microscope, because of this damned Summit.'

'Will we have to stay at the official residence in Rome?'

'Yes.'

'I don't like it there.'

'It's only for a short while.'

'Those receptions and banquets and dinners are so boring; how the hell do you expect me not to drink?'

He moved, so that he was between her and the mirror. 'I expect you to support me, as a wife,' he said.

She put down a mascara-stained ball of cotton wool.

'Haven't I always?'

'You have and I'm grateful,' said Billington. 'I just don't want there to be any mistakes. It's important.'

'For promotion, you mean?'

'Yes.'

'I won't do anything to hurt you,' she said solemnly.

'I love you,' he said.

'I love you too.'

'I'm sorry you're not happy.' The ambassador moved away from Fantani's view

'What about the jewellery?' she called after him. 'Shouldn't it be put away?'

Fantani winced. Distantly the man's voice said, 'In the morning.'

'Goodnight then,' she called.

'Goodnight.'

The light in the dressing room went out as abruptly as it had come on and Fantani tottered forward against the back of the couch to take the strain from his legs. He was thoroughly cramped, like he'd been sometimes as a child when the snows came to Calabria and the cold had eaten into his body, numbing him so badly it was difficult to walk. Still nervously alert for any sound, he lowered himself into a kneeling position, as if he were praying. He swallowed hard to prevent the sob, clamping his lips between his teeth against any breakdown. Gradually the spasms eased and he rolled over to rest his back against the rear of the couch.

It was two hours before Fantani considered it safe to move. He was fully recovered by then, as careful as he had been when he first entered. The ambassador had left the dressing-room door open. Fantani waited until he had located the man's slow, easy breathing and then padded swiftly across to the outer door. Soundlessly he tiptoed down the marble staircase and, when he got to the drawing-room windows, his hinged entry spots were as he had left them. In the garden he stopped, dragging the cold air into his lungs. Almost done it, he thought: almost but not quite. He found the cypress grove, and slipped swiftly down the utterly black avenue to the wall. At the cliff face he turned his back to the sea and paced five steps inland. Having established his marker he turned to the wall, cupped the silk bag in his hand and, like a basketball player going for a goal, hefted the jewellery high over the electrified barrier. With a sense of relief he heard it crunch on the other side.

Getting back was not going to be easy. The villa lights had been dimmed. There was no moon and, although he was close enough to reach out to feel its attachment to the wall,

104

he had to peer out to locate the blacker outline arching over the cliff. At least the breeze had dropped. Fantani breathed in deeply, tensed and threw himself into the blackness. He didn't land flat, as he had before, but instead jarred into the web with the left side of his body. He failed to get a foothold and for a second hung only by his left hand. He felt the grip being torn away by the weight of his body and swung his right hand around desperately for support.

And impaled his hand upon one of the spear heads.

He gasped at the pain, feeling the metal drive into his flesh. He pulled away, conscious of the skin ripping and managed to crook his almost numbed fingers around a spoke. His body hung suspended at the furthest point of the half-web and directly over the drop. He could feel the blood running back along his arm. He twitched his feet in tiny sideways movements to get a foothold. With his left foot he managed to lever himself up, sticking both arms through the bars and then curving them, so one hand was free to discover how badly hurt he was. The point had driven through the gloves, almost at the centre of the palm, like one of the sacrificial wounds in the church models of Jesus that his mother had made him pray before when he went to confession. He clamped his mouth shut against the moan. Dear God, it hurt; it hurt more than anything he'd ever known before. He was bleeding heavily and the fingers were stiffening. There was hardly any grip in his right hand, so he had to press his body tight against the sharpened tips. They scraped his face and he felt the cotton of his windcheater split. He made the turn and stopped again, his arms holding him. He couldn't manage it much longer: the numbness was spreading from his hand, into his wrist. He crabbed towards the cliff but pushed his body first this time. He got as far as his waist when his foot slipped and his legs slipped away from the metalwork, dangling over the edge. Fantani snatched out with his uninjured hand, locking his fingers into a bracken outcrop. He heaved up and, wedging his elbows beneath his body, dragged the rest of his body to safety.

He rolled away from the rim and lay on his back. He was crying at the effort, tears mixing with the sweat and itching his face. He let the emotion flood out, needing the release. He got up at last, pulling awkwardly with his left hand at the jacket zip and slotting his right arm into it, to create a makeshift sling. Reluctantly he went to the edge, paced in five steps and stopped, putting his good hand over the wet grass. He quickly located the jewellery and wedged it beneath his left arm.

The lightness of dawn was already showing to the east as he took the car along the Ostia road and then turned inland towards Rome. The feeling had practically gone from his hand and the lightheadedness he knew from marijuana and cocaine made him giggle aloud, careless at the closeness of hysteria. He'd done it!

The night-duty man contacted Harkness at home and the deputy decided the importance justified the use of an insecure line, telephoning the director in Hampshire. Wilson answered on the second ring.

'Sorry to disturb you,' Harkness said.

'What is it?'

'I asked for a deep investigation, beyond what we already had,' said the deputy. 'We've just had a response from Australia. It seems for a brief period Jill Walsingham was a member of the Communist party there.'

There was a short silence. Then Wilson demanded, 'Why's it taken so long to find out?'

'It was brief, like I said. Just three months, during her last year at university. Then she resigned.'

'Which is the first thing she would have been told to do, if she was going underground,' said Wilson. 'Did she know Walsingham then?'

'Not for another two years. They met when he was attached to Canberra.'

'So she could have sought him out, under instructions?'

'Yes.'

'So now the Walsinghams are more likely candidates than Semingford,' said the director.

During the night, he'd turned away from her. Charlie eased

himself around to avoid disturbing her. If she awoke she would want to make love and Charlie still had the ache of the previous night. The light was pale, hardly enough at first to create more than a silhouette. Clarissa slept on her back, with her mouth slightly parted. She was snoring, faint bubbly snores, and as he watched her face twitched, first into a frown and moments later into a smile. He wanted to reach out and touch her but held back.

What was he going to do about her?

There'd been affairs before, when Edith was alive, and she'd always been the excuse to end them, the person he'd gratefully returned home to. But now Edith was dead, so he didn't have his excuse. And he didn't know if he wanted one anyway.

Clarissa wore floppy hats to the Royal Enclosures at Ascot and crewed yachts during Cowes Week and ate from Fortnum and Mason hampers from the back of Rolls Royces at Glyndebourne. And he was Charlie Muffin, who had never got closer to Ascot than the betting shop in Dean Street, thought ocean racer was the name of a greyhound and had never known the difference between an aria and an intermezzo. No matter what she said to romanticize her adventure, it *was* a novelty – fun. It would be wrong to let his loneliness make it into anything more.

The telephone interrupted his thoughts. Charlie jumped, fumbling it from the rest to avoid awakening Clarissa. There was the echoing delay of an overseas connection and then the sound of Rupert Willoughby's voice.

Charlie hunched forward at the edge of the bed, his entire concentration upon what he was being told and its implications. He turned to see Clarissa blinking at him.

'What is it?' she said.

'There's been a robbery at the Billington villa,' said Charlie flatly. 'Everything's gone.'

She jerked up, so the bedclothes fell away from her. 'But that's ... '

' ... just too much of a coincidence,' completed Charlie.

'What are you talking about?' she said.

'I don't know,' said Charlie. 'Not yet.'

In London Rupert Willoughby stared down at the telephone and at the preliminary report of the inquiry agent which was alongside. He felt disgusted. At Clarissa. At Charlie. And at himself.

14

Early in his intelligence career Charlie Muffin developed an instinct, a personal antenna for danger. It had been instinct that turned him from the East Berlin border to hand the keys of the marked Volkswagen to a student to drive into a hail of machine-gun fire instead of an escape to the West. And it was the same instinct that gripped him now, as he went towards the villa at Ostia. He wasn't a clerk any more, making ticks against a piece of paper. He was Charlie Muffin, a renegade operative who had spent seven years hiding from any sort of authority, being forced to confront God knows how many police and a security system of a British embassy. And he *was* being forced. His initial thought in the Rome hotel room had been to run. But if he ran, less than twenty-four hours after completing an insurance survey during which he'd learned the security and opened the safe, he'd be the obvious suspect. And get no further than the first check at any airport he attempted to escape from. So there was only one thing he could do. Continue under the guise of insurance assessor and try to recover every scrap of the expertise he'd once had to avoid detection. It would be like trying to cross a fraying tightrope without a safety net; he never had liked circuses.

There was a police roadblock a mile from the villa, officialdom showing its stable-door mentality, but Charlie had taken the precaution of telephoning ahead, and after a radio check he was waved through. From the vantage point of the approaching hill the villa looked as if it were under siege by blue-uniformed carabinieri. They encircled the outside wall, apparently prodding through undergrowth for clues, and Charlie saw more moving in similar head-bent fashion throughout the stepped gardens. There were police everywhere. Rooflights flickered red, and from other cars came a distorted crackle of radios.

The gate check was more stringent than the one on the road and Charlie tensed at the scrutiny of his photograph against the Willoughby insurance authority and the recording of the hire-car number. The fear became a positive numbness, permeating his body. But they were all Italians here, so there was little risk of their identifying him. And it was still fifty-fifty with any of the embassy staff. If he were recognized at ground level he could give the same story he'd used with Willoughby: premature retirement because of policy changes. And hope to Christ no one was efficient enough to query it with London.

Before he was released at the gate, permission was sought by telephone from the main house in a babble of Italian and for some reason a policeman got into the passenger seat for the short journey to the villa. There were white sweat rings under the arms of his uniform and he had a machine pistol looped over his shoulder. The muzzle nudged against Charlie's leg when the man settled himself and Charlie waved it away. The man eyed him insolently but shifted slightly. He muttered something in Italian and Charlie said, 'Fuck you too.'

Nearer the house a concentration of uniformed and plain-clothes people were gathered by a wooden cradle, like the sort used on office blocks by window cleaners. It was slung over the cliff edge and men in overalls were strapped into it. They appeared to be examining a metal protection device shaped in a half circle.

Jane Williams was waiting for him. This time there was no offered hand.

'This is a terrible business,' she said.

'Yes,' said Charlie. Trouble always seemed to bring out the cliché in people.

'The ambassador is in his study.'

More men in uniform were assembled in some sort of guard outside the house, and as they went in Charlie saw plainclothes technicians working at a window area in one of the rooms off the central corridor.

'Who discovered it?' said Charlie.

'The ambassador.'

'How?'

'He went to the safe to replace some jewellery Lady Billington wore last night. And found it empty.'

'Any signs of entry?'

'Through one of the French windows back there.'

She stopped outside a door and said, 'Sir Hector's in there.'

The ambassador stood up at Charlie's entry, coming grave-faced towards him. He was a large man, tall and heavily built. His hair was cultivated long, for a patrician appearance, and if it hadn't been for the tan Charlie guessed he would be florid-faced. He must have modelled for the upstairs sculpture several years before. Billington wore white pumps, white trousers, and a silk cravat was immaculately knotted beneath a blue silk blazer. Charlie thought he looked ready to walk onto the set of one of those Fellini films he'd counted the minutes through in his early, conformist days in the department.

'Willoughby promised to contact you,' said the ambassador.

'Did he say why?'

'No,' said the ambassador. 'Have you met the police yet?'

'I wanted to see you first.'

Billington showed Charlie to a chair and sat himself behind a pristinely neat desk.

'Willoughby tells me everything has gone,' said Charlie.

'All except what my wife wore last night.'

'Why's that?'

'We'd been to a reception at the German embassy,' said Billington. 'Everything was intact when we left, at seven, because my wife had the safe open to choose what to wear. When I went to put it back this morning, it was empty. Everything gone.'

'How many staff have you got?'

'I've already told the police.'

'I'd like you to tell me,' pressed Charlie.

Billington hesitated and said, 'Nine.'

'They heard nothing?'

'Not a thing.'

'How was the safe opened?'

'It was opened!' said the ambassador, as if the question were ridiculous.

'By explosives? Or combination?' said Charlie patiently.

'Combination,' said Billington. 'The police say it was extremely professional.'

'Must have been,' said Charlie. 'I went through the whole system two days ago. Who had the combination?'

'What's that supposed to mean?' The ambassador bristled.

'It's supposed to mean I'm investigating the theft of a million and a half pounds' worth of jewellery,' said Charlie.

Billington coloured. 'Are you suggesting some member of my staff isn't trustworthy?'

'I'm suggesting that no thief is professional enough to bypass the security I saw, locate an unusually concealed safe and pick a combination lock like the one upstairs without some sort of help,' said Charlie. 'So who had the combination?'

'I did,' said Billington stiffly. 'My wife. The secretary. The embassy security man. There's a record of it in the security vault at the embassy. And my solicitor, of course, in London.'

'That's a lot of people,' said Charlie.

'All trustworthy.'

'Did anything happen which now seems to have been at all unusual, either here or at the embassy, immediately prior to the robbery?'

'Like what?'

'Anything you can think of.'

'No.' The response was categoric.

'What about afterwards? This morning for instance.'

'Why are you asking me this?' said Billington irritably.

'The jewellery is useless for any sort of normal disposal.'

'So what's the point of stealing it?'

'Resale to the insurers,' said Charlie. 'That's why

112

Willoughby was so anxious to stop me leaving Rome. He wants me to be here on the spot, ready to negotiate.'

Billington smiled for the first time, showing cosmetically even teeth. 'I suppose it's obvious,' he said. 'It's been such a confused morning it hadn't occurred to me.' He thought for a moment, then said, 'These negotiations you talk of, would they be independent of the police?'

'I doubt if they'd accept it,' said Charlie. 'Their interest is in an arrest.'

Billington looked doubtful. 'I'm not sure I could agree to bypass the authorities.'

'We're talking about jewellery you estimate to be worth two million pounds.'

'Which is adequately covered by an insurance policy that doesn't expire for another month,' reminded the ambassador. 'Obviously I'd like it back intact: some of the pieces are irreplaceable. And it would take years to build up a collection again.... '

Charlie hadn't anticipated Billington's opposition. 'I'd like you to think about it,' he said.

'One doesn't cooperate with criminals,' said Billington firmly.

'You wouldn't be,' said Charlie. 'I would.'

'I think you'd better tell Willoughby I'd like a settlement.'

'It's not as easy as that.'

'Why not?'

'Before we could consider any sort of settlement we would have to be absolutely satisfied about the circumstances of the robbery. And that there was no possibility of any of the articles being recovered,' said Charlie formally. He thought it sounded quite convincing.

'I'm not sure if I fully understand what you're implying,' said the ambassador.

'I'm not implying,' said Charlie. 'I am ensuring that you appreciate the terms of the policy.'

'I left that to my solicitor to negotiate,' said Billington.

'Then he should have made it clear that replacement is only considered when the police indicate there's no chance of recovery,' exaggerated Charlie. He supposed Billington could check with the lawyer but it was a chance he had to take.

'How long could that be?'

'I imagine the political embarrassment would prevent such an admission for a long time.'

'This is preposterous,' said Billington tightly. 'You're telling me I've virtually no cover!'

'Your cover is absolute and assured,' insisted Charlie. 'I've just set out the two ways it could be resolved, one quick, one protracted.'

'I'll have to give it some consideration.'

'Usually there isn't much delay in making an approach.'

'I'd be assured of your discretion?'

'Absolutely.' It was like gradually tiring a hooked fish, thought Charlie.

'It's not a situation I enjoy.'

'Who does?' said Charlie. 'But there are occasions when one has to be practical.'

'It *would* be a tragedy to lose some of the older pieces,' said Billington reflectively. 'They've been in the family for generations.'

'If there's an approach and we don't respond, it'll be broken down and sold piecemeal ... lost for ever.' Billington had almost given up fighting; it was time to slip the net beneath him and haul him in. There was a sudden knock at the door, and the chance was lost. Charlie looked up irritably. There was a man behind Jane Williams, dwarfing her with his bulk.

'Inspector Guilio Moro,' she said.

'Do you want to see me?' inquired Billington, rising to his feet.

'No,' said the policeman, pointing at Charlie. 'Him!'

The robbery report had come in less than an hour after the Australian information about Jill Walsingham. This time the duty officer awakened Sir Alistair Wilson and then sent a car, so the director arrived on the south side of the river earlier than normal. Harkness was already waiting when he got there.

'There's to be a meeting in Downing Street,' said the deputy. 'You're expected at eleven o'clock.'

Wilson had anticipated the summons. 'What do we know so far?'

'A robbery some time during the night,' said Harkness. 'There's extensive security precautions but all appear to have been bypassed. The safe is hidden in some peculiar way beneath a bureau or a desk or something. It was found easily enough, opened and cleaned out.'

'Of what?'

'Only jewellery: it's a private safe.'

'Carelessness isn't unusual: it's a leaky embassy,' said Wilson.

'Just jewellery,' assured Harkness.

'Our people involved?'

'Not directly,' said Harkness. 'I thought it best to keep the surveillance as it was. Walsingham has gone to the villa.'

Wilson got up and walked stiff-legged over to his river view, but did not bother to look out. 'What does it mean?'

'*Could* be coincidence.'

'Not a chance,' said Wilson positively. He stood still for a moment. 'What about the ambassador?'

'Sir Hector John Billington,' Harkness read from his file. 'Father – Sir John Billington, who was ambassador to Washington and Paris before returning to the Foreign Office as Permanent Under Secretary in the late forties. The son was brilliant. Got a Triple First in Greats at Oxford and a law degree, which isn't the usual combination. Entered the diplomatic service a year earlier than his father, passed every internal examination with honours, usually a year and sometimes two ahead of the normally expected period. Junior posting to Washington, with distinction, first ambassadorship to Saudi Arabia. Big impact there. Credited on an internal memorandum with greatly influencing the Saudi court in maintaining a moderate stance and keeping oil prices down through OPEC. From Saudi Arabia he went to Brussels. Difficult time in Belgium explaining our reduced defence support for NATO, particularly as the Common

Market is headquartered there. After Brussels posted to Rome. He's been there two years.'

Wilson picked up the inconsistency immediately. 'Why Rome?' he said. 'Billington's obviously a Foreign Office star. Rome is a backwater.'

Harkness smiled. 'I had the same thought,' he said 'He's rising *too* fast. There's a log jam of seniority above him. When the retirements come, in a year or two, he'll get the prime postings, either Paris or Washington.'

'What about the wife?'

'Lady Billington's family name is Hethenton,' said Harkness. 'Father was Lord Mendale. The fortune is put at ten million but that's only a guess: tax lawyers and accountants have got it so well spread it could be that much again.'

Wilson began his aimless stumping around the office again. 'We know they've got Hotovy.' He was thinking aloud. 'They've obviously broken him.'

'But he didn't know the reason for the inquiry,' reminded Harkness. 'So what can he tell them? Just that he found the origin of a message was Cape Town. By itself that's meaningless.'

'I still can't go along with coincidence,' said Wilson.

The internal telephone sounded. Because he was nearer, Harkness answered. 'The car's waiting for you downstairs,' he said.

'Thanks.'

'They're going to want some answers.'

'I haven't got any,' said Wilson.

The Prime Minister's residence in Downing Street has several entrances. There is the obvious and public front door or the less conspicuous corridor from the official house of the Chancellor of the Exchequer next door. The most discreet is at the back, from Horseguards Parade and across the gardens and this was the route that Sir Alistair used. The patterned hand of the Ministry of Works was obvious from the scrupulous flower arrangements. Wilson looked for roses and was disappointed.

Naire-Hamilton was already waiting in the downstairs

ante-room. He hurried up at the director's entry. He was flushed more than Wilson could remember seeing him, the redness suffusing even his balding head.

'What on earth's happening?' demanded the Permanent Under Secretary.

'You've read the early account of the robbery?'

'Of course.'

'Then you know as much as I do.'

The door opened suddenly and a secretary beckoned them forward. Wilson deferred politely to Naire-Hamilton, following him to the Prime Minister's first-floor study. It overlooked St James's Park and the rose beds; perhaps that's why they didn't bother with them in the immediate garden, thought the director idly.

The Secret Intelligence Service comes under the direct control of the Foreign Secretary, with ultimate responsibility held by the Premier. Both men were waiting for them. George Ramsay was a thick-set, bespectacled man who had won the previous election largely through personal appeal as the blunt-talking man of the people who would neither mislead the electorate with monetary gymnastics to achieve economic miracles nor allow unions to abuse their powers. Even Ramsay, a consummately professional politician, had been surprised by the reaction to the straight-from-the-shoulder approach recommended by the advertising agency who masterminded the campaign. Ramsay cultivated the image of the Prime Minister who had come to power after a divisive period of British politics to introduce stability. He worked hard to sustain the role, because basically he enjoyed it. He sported chain-store suits and smoked a reassuring pipe. Occasionally the plain speaking was overwhelmed with Welsh rhetoric and a fondness for cliché. A favourite metaphor had him as the captain guiding a troubled ship from storms into calmer water: another was the need to avoid rocking the boat. He was at his desk when Naire-Hamilton and Wilson entered. The pipe was alight and he wore cardigan and slippers. The intelligence director didn't think he looked much like a captain: more like a clever MP on his way to a fancy-dress party.

'Don't like this,' announced Ramsay at once.

Obviously plain-speaking time, decided the director.

'It's going to cause a lot of publicity. Can't have that, with the other business,' supported Ian Beldon. The Foreign Secretary entered politics from Cambridge, where he'd had the Chair of Philosophy. It was difficult to imagine him as an academic. He was a burly, red-faced man of heavy, ponderous movement. Rumour was that he was the cabinet bully and Wilson found the accusation easy to believe.

Wilson had expected the Permanent Under Secretary to lead but Naire-Hamilton turned, inviting the response from him. 'There's got to be a connection,' said the director.

'What?' demanded Ramsay.

'At this stage I don't know.'

'We don't seem to know much about anything do we?' said Beldon.

'We only confirmed the origin of the leak a week ago,' said the director, annoyed at the attack. I was instructed to conduct a cautious, discreet inquiry.'

Ramsay got up from his desk and went to an adjoining table, to knock the dottle from his pipe. The slippers were the type without heels, so he shuffled across the carpet. Ramsay worked with a pipe cleaner. It was several minutes before he appeared satisfied. He turned back to the two men and said, 'The risk now is that everything is going to come out.'

'We're fully aware of the situation,' said Naire-Hamilton, entering the discussion at last.

'I'm not going to be made to look stupid,' insisted the Premier. 'Unless this is settled – and settled as I want it to be – I can't lead the delegation to Rome in a fortnight's time . . . no one can go. . . . '

'No,' said Naire-Hamilton.

'And we can't cancel either,' said Beldon.

'So what are you going to do?' demanded Ramsay.

Again the Permanent Under Secretary gave Wilson his cue. 'There are two possible lines of inquiry,' said the director, uncomfortable with the words as he uttered them.

'Possible? Or positive?' seized Ramsay, with a politician's ability to discern an empty sentence.

'Only possible,' admitted Wilson.

'That's not very encouraging,' said the Foreign Secretary.

'There's a filter on anything sensitive going into the embassy, and I've got six men inside, under cover of Summit preparations, and a separate surveillance team of a further twelve,' said Wilson.

'What exactly have they come up with?' said Beldon.

'The inquiry has only just started.'

'You've already said that.' Beldon wasn't going to make this easy.

'We accept the difficulties,' interceded Ramsay. 'But it's got to be settled.' He paused. 'That's why I want you to go personally.'

'Me!' said Wilson.

'I know it's not usual, but the circumstances aren't usual. Before I can set foot in that embassy, I've got to know it's scoured clean.'

'I see the point,' said Naire-Hamilton.

'Glad you do,' said Ramsay. 'I want you to go too.'

Naire-Hamilton's hands rose and fell, like frightened birds seeking a spot to land. 'But that's not.... '

' ... usual, I know,' the Premier interrupted. 'We've already discussed that. I want Wilson here solving the security problems and I want you cementing over the cracks. I want to go to Italy in a fortnight's time with only the Summit to worry about.... ' He smiled, a politician imparting a confidence. 'Believe me, that's going to be enough.'

Naire-Hamilton looked like he was standing to attention on a parade ground. It was anger, Wilson decided; this temporary inspector had altered the bus route more drastically than was permitted and Naire-Hamilton was offended. 'If that's your wish,' he said, brittle-voiced.

'No,' said Ramsay, relighting his pipe, 'it's not my wish: it's my instruction. You've got a week, at most. I'm laying on RAF transport at Northolt for whatever needs you have. I'm entrusting you with full authority; all I want to know is that it's been cleared up.'

Naire-Hamilton's car was waiting in Horseguards Road, by the park. He strode angrily towards it around the edge of the parade ground, head forward. Wilson had to step out to keep pace, which was difficult with his lame leg.

'Who the hell does he think he is!' exclaimed Naire-Hamilton.

'The Prime Minister,' said Wilson simply.

'Damned upstart.'

15

The ambassador directed them to the reception room in which Charlie had been abandoned by Jane Williams on his first visit. There was a palatial embarrassment of space. The two men regarded each other warily, Charlie trying to conceal his apprehension. Inspector Moro was a pear-shaped shambles of a man. His clothes were a contradiction of effort; the shirt bubbled apart from the strain of each fastening and the crumpled silk suit that enveloped him looked like a cast-off from someone even larger. The heat troubled him, despite the air conditioning, so he frequently dabbed a once-white handkerchief around his face and inside the neckband of his shirt. Charlie's impression was of a bloated python sweating to shed a skin.

'You didn't take long getting here.'

'I was already in Rome,' said Charlie.

'I know.'

'So why the surprise?'

'No surprise: just curious.'

Charlie recognized that there was nothing scruffy about the questioning. Moro was conducting the interrogation exactly as he would have done in the circumstances, hard and sharp. The policeman's English was immediate, without any pause for the right word.

'Why curious?' said Charlie.

'You spend two days here, looking at the security and the collection. And then there's a robbery,' said Moro. 'If you were a policeman, wouldn't you be curious?'

'I suppose so,' conceded Charlie. 'Except that I'm here

at the villa and not on some plane going in the opposite direction.'

'You wouldn't have made it.'

'What?'

'The plane. I closed every airport against you four hours ago.'

Thank Christ he hadn't tried to run, thought Charlie; but the numbing, cotton-wool-in-the-head feeling was making an uncomfortable return. 'Satisfied?' he said. He hoped his nervousness didn't show.

'No.'

'Why not?'

'It would be cleverer to come back, wouldn't it?'

'I'm not involved,' insisted Charlie. Would the policeman already have made an identity check through the Interpol communications link? Charlie felt the sweat prick out on his back.

'Convince me,' said Moro.

'How?'

'Tell me how a security system as impregnable as this was so easily breached.'

'I would have thought that was obvious.'

'Perhaps it isn't to me.'

'It can't possibly be an outside job,' said Charlie. 'There has to be inside knowledge of the alarms and the position of the safe.'

'Which you knew.'

'So did at least six other people, apart from the staff.'

'Hardly impregnable, was it?' said Moro.

'No.'

'Which could be expensive for you, either way.'

'Either way?'

'If you've got to pay out as a genuine insurer. Or if you're involved. Because there's no way you're going to get out of Italy.'

The nausea swept through Charlie, so that he actually belched. He hadn't expected the confrontation to be easy, but he hadn't expected this sort of hostility either.

Moro made a sweeping gesture with his hand. 'I haven't

investigated a crime for a long time,' he said. 'Not even a crime of this size.'

'So what are you doing here?'

'My job!'

'What's that?'

'Diplomatic protection.'

Which accounted for the perfect English, thought Charlie. 'What's diplomatic about this?'

'By tomorrow the newspapers here and abroad will be saying we can't protect foreign politicians and diplomats, any more than the government can do anything effective to stamp out terrorism. Our subversive groups are quick to see a trend. We can't take the risk, with the Summit.'

'What Summit?' said Charlie. Uncertainty was piling upon uncertainty.

'In two weeks' time Italy is hosting a Common Market and NATO Summit,' said Moro.

The department wouldn't be directly involved, calculated Charlie. But there would be a watching brief, with all the protection intelligence channelled for routine information. And that would extend to photographs. Charlie thrust his hands deeply into his pockets, clenching his fists until his fingers hurt, to stop the nervous shaking.

'I understand your problem,' he said.

'I'm not sure that you do.'

Supercilious bastard, thought Charlie. 'I'm sure you'll explain it,' he said.

The mockery got through to the Italian, his lip tightening against his teeth. 'My orders from the Prime Minister's office are to stop the trend, before it begins,' he said. 'And that means an arrest. So I'm going to get one.'

'Which should save my company a lot of money.'

'I'm not interested in saving your money.'

'What are you interested in?'

'Catching who did it.'

'So?'

'You want to recover what was stolen, to minimize your liability.'

'Isn't that the same?'

123

'Don't be smart,' said Moro. 'I know how these robberies are usually settled with insurance companies. Some black-car meeting in an alley with a ransom exchange. But that isn't going to happen here. If there's any contact for a percentage settlement I want to know about it. I want to know the time it's made, when the meeting is arranged and I don't care how much of the jewellery is lost in the process.'

Bollocks, thought Charlie.

'Do you understand what I'm saying?'

'You speak the language well enough,' said Charlie.

'Try it any other way and there'll still be an arrest. It'll be yours, for impeding inquiries. And, if I find you've paid over any money, the charge will be complicity to rob.'

'Loud and clear,' said Charlie.

Moro smiled unexpectedly. It had the effect of puddling the fat on his cheeks. 'I'm not intending it to be one-sided,' said the detective, as a sudden concession. 'For cooperation from you, there'll be cooperation from me. I'll show you the safe first.'

Moro had an odd rolling gait, as if his weight needed constant balancing, but he moved through the house with an immediate familiarity. There were police on guard outside both bedrooms leading to the dressing area. Moro entered through Billington's door. There were more men inside, heads bent in the hunt for clues like those in the garden. The bed was unmade and Billington's pyjamas were draped over a pillow. The examination of the dressing room had been completed and it was empty of forensic scientists. The area around the safe was white from fingerprint powder.

'Absolutely clean,' said the Italian.

Charlie raised his eyebrows. Stooping he saw they had even tested the securing bolt at the rear of the sideways-moving pedestal. 'I've never known an installation like this,' he said.

'Neither have I.'

'So it wouldn't be an obvious place to look.'

'No.'

'What about entry?' said Charlie.

'Downstairs sitting room,' said Moro.

There was more fingerprint powder around the French windows and sticky tape acted as hinges on two cleanly cut panes, one near the lock and another low, adjacent to the breaker alarm nipples. There were bypass clips still linking them.

'What about them?' asked Charlie.

'Two thousand lire in any electrical shop in the city,' said Moro.

Wind was gusting in from the sea, dissipating the oppressive midday heat. Moro's hair lifted in the breeze, tousling untidily around his perspiring face. The two men walked out onto the verandah, and looked out towards the men suspended over the cliff in the window cleaner's hoist.

'It can't have been easy,' said Charlie.

'It wasn't,' said Moro. 'One of them must be quite badly hurt. It happened on the way out, otherwise there would have been bloodstains inside the house. There's a lot of blood on the metalwork and smeared against the grass on the other side. We'll be able to get a grouping and at least part if not all of a palm print.'

'It's a hand injury?'

'Looks like it,' said Moro. He pointed to one of the spear-shaped points. 'We think he caught himself, trying to get around that. Clothes were torn, too. We've got a lot of fibres for comparison.'

Moro turned away from the forensic examination to look directly at Charlie. 'What's your insured value?'

'One and a half million sterling,' said Charlie.

Impassive, Moro made an entry into a notebook with a surprisingly small gold pen. The writing was neat and precise. 'I'm going to limit all the information,' said Moro. 'I don't want you making any press releases.'

Publicity was the last thing Charlie wanted. 'Don't worry,' he said.

'At the moment you know as much as I do,' said Moro.

'Which isn't much,' said Charlie.

'Remember what I said.'

'How could I forget?'

'You'd better not,' said Moro.

Emilio Fantani's hand had been stitched and then strapped across his body so that the damaged palm was practically upright against his left shoulder. There had been an injection against both the pain and infection but the Italian was still whey-faced, wincing at occasional spasms.

'The police will check hospitals and doctors,' warned Solomatin. The injury was unforeseen and Solomatin was unsettled by it: the plan had been perfect and now it was flawed.

'The doctor's a queer,' said Fantani, tight-lipped in his discomfort. 'I've got photographs that could ruin him.'

Solomatin felt the anxiety lessen slightly. 'What about fingerprints?'

'The fingers of the gloves remained intact,' said Fantani.

Solomatin smiled briefly. 'You did well,' he said.

'What have you done with it?'

'All safe,' assured Solomatin. In the deposit box with the other material that was going to switch suspicion. Hiding it in the box hadn't been part of Kalenin's plan and Solomatin was uneasy at the improvisation.

Fantani looked at his bandaged hand. 'The tendons could be affected,' he said. 'The doctor made me try to move my fingers and I couldn't.'

'Bruising,' said Solomatin. 'It'll be all right.' The man would be dead before he had the chance.

'You know where the insurance man is?'

Solomatin nodded. 'It won't be long now.'

'How long?'

'Two days; three at the most.'

Fantani tried to flex his injured hand. 'Hurts like hell,' he said.

'All you have to do is arrange one meeting,' said Solomatin. 'I'll do the rest; I'll even carry the stuff to the exchange spot.'

'Where?' demanded Fantani.

'An apartment on the Via Salaria.'

'Apartment?'

'I'm going to move people in,' said Solomatin. 'To cover the exchange.'

Fantani felt reassured by the promise of protection. 'We're going to work together now, aren't we?' he said, anxious for the commitment.

'Hand in glove,' smiled the Russian. It was a bad joke, but Fantani smiled.

In the censored society of Moscow, ambiguous phrases and expressions have evolved to convey happenings which are never officially announced. Criticism on Tass or in *Pravda* or *Isvestia* of the failure of a programme or an announced development plan is usually the first hint of a purge against the man in charge. Sometimes, though not often, the victim is named, so as to remove any vestige of doubt. If there isn't identification in the first instance, it usually comes from the disclosure of some illness or other to account for an absence during any public event. With Boris Kastanazy the procedure was different. His secret position with the KGB prevented any criticism of work failure, so the suggestion of ill health was unexpected and initially confused the Western embassies who monitor and attempt to interpret such statements.

Valery Kalenin wasn't confused. He put the newspaper aside and lit one of his tubed cigarettes. The place was vacant on the Politburo. He intended it to be his.

16

It was an irrational impression, standing on a clifftop overlooking hundreds of miles of open sea, but Charlie was gripped by a feeling of constriction, of being enclosed. And he was enclosed, as securely as if he had been inside the four walls of a jail. His name would be on file now, the description fed into the computers, ready to be spewed out at the touch of a button. Charlie tried to breathe out against the surge of panic. There'd been moments of danger in the past seven years, but he'd never come under this degree of official scrutiny. Moro had started out treating him as a suspect and Charlie knew the detective wasn't completely satisfied, despite the apparent willingness to cooperate. It would only need one computer print-out punched into another and the lights would go on like Christmas decorations.

Charlie walked back through the cypress grove, the sickness bunched in his stomach. 'Shit!' he said vehemently. 'Shit!'

The search squads had worked up through the gardens and were milling around in the driveway with nothing to do. Some lounged against cars and others squatted at the grass edge, smoking and talking. A police vehicle had been driven in behind his car and the radio was on like those near the gate lodge, so the stutter of conversation was overlaid by bursts of static-strained talk between controllers and radio operators. Robbery or no robbery, Charlie didn't think it would take long for the ambassador to become annoyed at his property being trampled over by half the police feet in Italy.

Charlie entered through the side door. Police crowded the

128

corridor, using the fish-mouthed fountain as a gathering point. Lady Billington was at the foot of the staircase, looking around her in bemusement at the activity. Her face relaxed when she recognized Charlie. 'Would you believe all these people!'

She was carrying one of the cats and Charlie got the impression it arched its back towards him.

'I'm sorry,' said Charlie.

'They're not with you, are they?'

'I meant about the robbery.'

She put her head to one side. 'I wondered what it would be like not having them, didn't I?' she said. 'Now I know.'

'What's it feel like?'

'Nothing,' she said. 'Actually it's you I feel sorry for; you've got to pay.'

One way or another, thought Charlie. He said, 'What happened exactly?'

'I was dressing when Hector came in to put away last night's jewellery. He opened the safe and said, "Oh my God!" Every case we opened was empty.'

'You heard nothing during the night?'

'Not a thing.' She shuddered. 'Don't like the idea of some awful man going through my things. They will be caught, won't they?'

'The police seem very determined.'

'You thought the security was adequate.'

'Everyone did.'

'Hector's dreadfully upset.'

'He's waiting for me now,' said Charlie, excusing himself.

There was someone else in Billington's study.

'Wanted to talk your idea through with Henry Walsingham,' said Billington. 'Security.'

Momentarily Charlie was shielded by the ambassador. It lasted seconds but there was a bizarre, slow-motion surrealism about Walsingham's approach. Charlie was confronted by a pale-faced man, with blond, near-white hair, a matching, drooped moustache and a stridently checked three-piece suit. Walsingham shook hands with a stiff, hinge-in-the-neck sort of movement that reminded Charlie of the national

129

service subalterns who'd made him scrub coalhouses with a toothbrush. A stranger, decided Charlie, relieved: he was sure they'd never met before. But his stomach was still moving, loose-bowelled.

'The more I think about it, the unhappier I become,' declared Billington, returning to his desk after the formalities were over.

'A sell-back was Inspector Moro's first thought,' said Charlie, taking the chair to the left of the desk. Walsingham sat in front, back upright, one leg crossed over the other. The trouser creases were sharp-edged and the brogues glimmered. Charlie recognized a hot-spoon job.

'Is he happy about it?' said the ambassador.

'Hardly,' said Charlie. 'But he didn't oppose it.'

'What then?'

'He knows it's the most likely way the thieves will choose and wants us to work together.' An idea began to form in Charlie's mind; it had a conceited desperation about it, but it was feasible.

'Are there any clues?' The security man had a thin, weak voice.

'A lot on the cliff,' said Charlie. 'One of them was injured getting around the metal protection. There's sufficient blood for grouping. There are some clothes fibres, trapped on the spikes and at least one palm print.'

'I think we can leave it to the police,' said Billington.

'The police *want* me to negotiate,' said Charlie. 'They've got enough for a conviction, not an arrest. That will come from the insurance arrangement.'

'It would be unseemly for an ambassador of the Crown to deal with thugs.' Billington retreated to his basic objection.

'You don't have to be involved,' repeated Charlie. 'All you have to do is wait for the contact. And tell me.' As quickly as possible, so I can get the hell out of it.

'You will liaise with the police?'

'I've given Inspector Moro that undertaking.' That was an exaggeration too, but Billington was on the hook again and this time Charlie couldn't afford to lose him.

'What do you think?' the ambassador asked Walsingham.

130

'I think official approval from the police is essential,' the man replied guardedly.

'Which I have,' said Charlie. There wasn't any point in buggering about with half-truths any more. Speed was what mattered.

'Then I suppose it would be all right.' Walsingham was still doubtful.

'I'll pass on any initial contact,' agreed Billington suddenly. 'But that's all.'

'That's all I want.'

'From that moment I don't want any part of what follows. You'll liaise entirely through Walsingham here. And, if there's a return or whatever, you're to handle it; nothing more to do with me.'

Typical bloody commander, thought Charlie, back at base camp out of the firing while everyone else gets their asses shot off. Beside him Walsingham uncrossed his legs and placed his bright shoes at attention. 'What would you want me to do?' he said to Charlie.

And you're the sort of silly sod who marches off to the front whistling 'Colonel Bogey', thought Charlie; he decided the man's moustache would make soup hazardous. 'Contact numbers would be useful,' he said.

The security man took a worn leather wallet from inside his jacket and Charlie half saw a faded regimental crest. Walsingham handed him a card with his private number as well as an embassy telephone listing.

'Is that all?' Walsingham was clearly disappointed.

'Until there *is* any approach, there can't be anything else, can there?' said Charlie. Through the perpetual apprehension came the feeling of satisfaction he always got at winning.

'I don't want this to become embarrassing,' insisted Billington.

'Neither do I,' said Charlie. All Billington had to lose was one and a half million pounds' worth of shiny stones. Charlie had much more.

There was a Lancia interchanging with a Fiat behind him on the return drive from Ostia. It would be the police, Charlie knew. It would be wrong to overreact to Moro. If he let his nerves respond to every development like a bell-striker on a fairground ring-your-strength machine, he was going to create precisely the suspicion he was attempting to avoid. He was at the sharp end of a difficult situation. But he'd been in worse and got out. . . .

Clarissa wasn't at the hotel when he returned and Charlie was relieved. She was another problem that had to be solved. When he was working, properly working, Charlie didn't like distractions. The robbery could be the excuse he had been looking for in bed that morning.

Charlie listened to Willoughby's London number being dialled and was conscious of the concern in the underwriter's voice when he came on the line. The embarrassment that Charlie felt at their earlier contact wasn't there any more.

'How bad is it?' demanded Willoughby.

'Bad,' said Charlie. He gave a swift but complete account and when he finished Willoughby said, 'There's obviously a thief on the ambassador's staff.'

'Not obviously,' said Charlie. 'But possibly.'

'You warned Billington of an approach?'

'Yes,' said Charlie. 'He's not keen.'

'On recovering everything intact!'

'He's worried that any personal involvement would compromise him,' said Charlie. 'He's talking about a settlement.'

'That wouldn't be easy,' said Willoughby.

'What do you mean?'

'I mean two million pounds.'

He was going with Alice through the looking-glass and the room was getting smaller again. 'Didn't you spread the cover?' said Charlie wearily. Just like Hong Kong and the liner fire.

'No.'

'I didn't think gambling and insurance went hand in hand,' said Charlie.

'I needed liquidity,' said Willoughby. 'Whoever would have thought Billington's stuff could be stolen?'

'Whoever took it,' said Charlie unhelpfully.

'What about obviation of policy if there isn't a sell-back?' said Willoughby.

'Not a chance.' Charlie would not give the man false hope. 'I confirmed every item on the list twenty-four hours before it was taken. And there hadn't been the slightest alteration to the protection as it's described. You're one hundred and one per cent liable.'

'Thanks a million.'

'Two million,' corrected Charlie.

'Is there any point in my coming out?'

Charlie glanced towards the closet where Clarissa's clothes were tight-packed. 'I don't think so,' he said. 'Not yet.'

'You've managed difficult things before.'

'Not like this,' said Charlie. He needed all the luck he could get.

In London Willoughby looked across the room towards the safe in which the observation reports were locked. He wouldn't use them, he decided. He'd wait for another occasion to trap Clarissa. And knowing her it wouldn't take long.

Henry Jackson was already waiting when Wilson and Naire-Hamilton entered the suite that had been established as a communal briefing room.

'An up-to-date summary,' demanded Wilson crisply.

'We let Walsingham go out to the villa as instructed,' said Jackson. 'He got back to the embassy about an hour ago. We've spoken by telephone. He says the police believe there was inside help. From our own observation we identified police being moved in to watch the villa staff and put a cover on all embassy personnel with frequent access.'

'What about the embassy?'

'Not the panic that I'd hoped for. And I've had our people making a bloody nuisance of themselves to Walsingham and Semingford.'

'What's the security like?' asked Naire-Hamilton.

'Walsingham gave me a tour,' said Jackson. 'Seemed tight enough.'

'You advised the embassy of my arrival?' said Wilson.
'Half an hour ago.'
'Let's see if I can shake the trees,' said Wilson.

17

Clarissa sensed Charlie's mood. She didn't speak in the lift, but outside the hotel on the Via Sistina she looped both hands through his arm and hugged against him. Charlie glanced towards the Spanish Steps and isolated the un-marked police car with its boot-mounted aerial. He moved off in the opposite direction.

'Why are we walking?' she said.

'Good for us,' said Charlie. When the moment had come in the hotel room he'd ducked it, like a bloody fool. It wasn't going to get any easier.

She pulled closer to him but didn't say anything.

The Via Sistina is a street of small shops, none very fashionable, but Charlie went through the charade of stopping and staring and quickly identified the man following them in the reflection of a boutique window. He was small, in a double-breasted suit and a wide-brimmed hat, which was identifiable and made him an amateur at surveillance.

For positive confirmation Charlie crossed suddenly near the road junction by the theatre, as if he wanted to check the programme. The man darted after them. Clarissa was curious but said nothing.

With all the determination of the committed sightseer, which is what he wanted to appear in the subsequent reports to Moro, Charlie set a course for the Trevi fountain, the nearest landmark he could think of. There was the usual throng of tourists around the base of the monument when they arrived in the square. Clarissa immediately demanded a coin.

135

'To make a wish work you've got to stand with your back to the fountain,' Charlie said.

She did as she was instructed, closed her eyes and tossed the coin awkwardly over her head. Quickly glancing sideways Charlie saw the blue-suited man at the side parapet where the horse-drawn carriages were parked waiting for tourist fares.

'Now you,' said Clarissa.

'Can't afford it,' said Charlie. Irritated with himself, he took her arm, guiding her through the crowd up to the higher balustrade. As they walked, Charlie saw one of the carriage horses start to urinate in a sudden, steaming burst, and from the way the policeman jumped Charlie guessed he hadn't been able to get his feet out of the way in time.

There was a small café, with three tables wedged onto the pavement, but they were all occupied. It was cramped in the dark interior and smelled of yesterday's garlic. Charlie ordered cognac with his coffee but predictably Clarissa refused alcohol. They sat unspeaking until the drinks were served and then Clarissa said, 'Why not say it?'

'I don't want you to stay.'

'I know.'

'You could be in Menton by tonight.'

'I don't want to go to Menton.'

'I'm working.'

'And I'm in the way.'

Charlie swirled the liquor around the tiny balloon glass. 'Something isn't right,' he said.

'What do you mean.'

'The robbery isn't right. I don't know what it is. . . .'

'You aren't making sense.'

'Nothing makes sense at the moment.'

'I still don't see why I can't stay with you.'

'I don't think it's safe.'

'That sounds dramatic.'

'We were followed here. By the police.'

Clarissa stared wildly around the café. 'Good Lord!'

'What happens if they check with Rupert in London?'

'I don't know.'

136

'Of course you bloody know.'

'Don't shout.'

'I'm sorry. Just go. Please.'

'Slam, bam, thank you, ma'am?'

'Your rules.'

'You played.'

'And now the game is over?'

'It isn't just that, is it?' She put her hand on his arm. Charlie could not hold the stare from the clear blue eyes.

'Unless we're sensible this is going to end up a real mess,' he said.

'So what?'

'I don't want it. For Rupert. Or for you.'

'So what are you going to do?'

'I don't know.'

'You ran away after America.'

'Yes.' There was no doubt he had a talent for it.

'Don't run away this time.'

'I'd like you to leave,' he said doggedly.

Clarissa sighed. 'I'm disappointed, Charlie.'

'I didn't make any promises.'

'It wasn't promises I wanted.'

'What then?'

She considered an answer and then appeared to change her mind. 'Don't come back to the hotel with me,' she said.

'All right.'

'See you in London,' she said and Charlie knew she meant it. He said nothing.

He followed her as far as the café door. As she walked away, Charlie watched men's heads turn and he felt pride, not jealousy. The blue-suited detective shifted and then relaxed again against the balustrade overlooking the fountain. Charlie saw someone else move away from the crowd. It could have been coincidence, because there was a constant flow of people along the approach roads, but he didn't think it was. The man was wearing a grey suit and Charlie had the feeling he had seen him before.

The meal began in frigid silence, like all the others. After a few moments Semingford pushed his plate away, food untouched.

'Something wrong?'

'No.'

'What then?' Ann Semingford was an angular, sharp-featured woman who had responded to her husband's neglect by neglecting herself. The smock dress was the one she had been wearing for most of the week and her hair hung lankly around a face that was shiny without make-up.

'I'm not hungry.'

'Love!'

'I want to talk.'

'That'll make a change.'

'I want a divorce, Ann.'

She stopped eating. 'The moment of truth!' she said, striking a pose.

'Don't be stupid.'

'Isn't it you who's being stupid?'

'What's the point of either of us bothering?'

'You know how I feel about divorce.'

'That's hypocritical, in the circumstances. Do you want me just to walk out?'

'I don't think you'd do that, Richard. It would hardly help your career, would it?'

'Bugger my career.'

'Since when?'

'It isn't important any more.'

'What is?'

'Finding a way to be with Jane.'

18

Sir Alistair Wilson entered the embassy through the main entrance off the Via Settembre, identified himself at the reception area and signed in. Walsingham appeared within minutes, hurrying across the marble vestibule. He was heavier jowled than he appeared in the personnel photographs, with the beginning of a paunch corseted by the waistcoat of a brown-checked suit.

'Sir Alistair Wilson?' said Walsingham tentatively.

Wilson extended his hand. Walsingham's response was wet-palmed.

'I've told the ambassador you were coming,' he said eagerly.

'Thank you,' said Wilson. The security officer appeared more nervous than Wilson would have expected.

'He said to let him know if you wanted to see him.' Walsingham hesitated and added, 'Actually he was surprised you hadn't approached him.'

'Is there an office we can go to?' said Wilson.

The abruptness seemed to unsettle Walsingham even further. He hesitated and then said, 'Certainly.'

Wilson walked in silence along the echoing corridor, conscious of the occasional look of curiosity from people they passed. It had clearly been a minor palace in the past and Wilson admired the gracious marble and panelling. Walsingham's office was on the second floor, at the rear of the building, overlooking the Via Cernaia. Wilson noted the soldierly tidiness about everything.

'I was in the middle of preparing the report when I heard you were coming,' said Walsingham.

139

'About what?'

'The robbery, of course. That's why you're here, isn't it?'

The man was very much on edge. Wilson didn't think Walsingham would have made a good interrogator: which was probably why he'd been passed over twice for promotion. 'No,' he said.

'I thought Mr Jackson was supervising the Summit arrangements?'

'He is.'

Walsingham smiled feebly. 'I'm afraid I don't understand.'

'Did you know your wife was a member of the Communist party in Australia?' said Wilson sharply.

Walsingham made an indeterminate sound, somewhere between a laugh and a grunt of disbelief. 'Of course I knew.'

'It's not on the antecedent records. Or in the personnel file.'

'It was when she was at school, for God's sake! Imagined herself in love with some student and joined because he did, to be in the same place. The membership ended when the romance did. She thought they were a lot of bloody fools, rushing about with banners protesting about the Vietnam war.'

'It wasn't recorded.'

'Because neither of us thought anything about it. I belonged to the Scouts but I didn't record that.'

'You were an officer cadet, too. You put that down.'

'Because it was relevant to my going into the army and not directly joining the diplomatic service.'

'Who decided to leave it out, you or she?'

'I can't remember.'

'Try.'

Walsingham's hand was at his face, as if the skin irritated. 'I really can't remember. It was not a conscious decision, something we discussed.'

'But it was,' said Wilson. 'She told you about it in the first place.'

'Not about belonging to some daft organization. It was one of those honesty things; admitting all the previous romances, so we would start married life without any secrets. It was the student she told me about: the party membership was incidental. Didn't you do that sort of thing with your wife?'

'No,' said Wilson coldly.

'Surely you haven't come all the way from London to ask me about something as unimportant as that!' said Walsingham. The nervousness had melted into outrage.

'Perhaps it isn't unimportant.'

'Ask my wife.'

'Why don't we?'

Walsingham's fifth-floor apartment was situated near the river, in an old building without a lift. The staircase spiralled around the walls, creating an open central tunnel down which it was possible to look from the top to the bottom. They climbed in hostile silence. Walsingham had asked to telephone, but Wilson forbade it, not wanting to permit the woman any preparation.

'Here we are.' There was the sound of a radio playing inside the apartment.

Taking immediate control, Wilson pushed Walsingham aside and knocked. Jill Walsingham was a plump, sagging woman. Flesh bulged beneath her jeans and she wasn't wearing a bra: the T-shirt strained with the effort. She had a roller crimped on either side of her head, so that she appeared to be wearing some odd sort of hat, and her face was clear of make-up. There was a brief frown of surprise. Then she smiled and said, 'What are you doing here?'

'I'm not sure,' said Walsingham.

She stood back to let them enter. It was a large apartment, with a view of the Tiber from an outside balcony. The drapes were velvet and reached the floor, which was thickly carpeted. The furniture was heavy but the room was big enough to allow it; Wilson noted that the couch and chairs were antique. The oil paintings either side of the fireplace were School of Tintoretto and the mantlepiece clock was eighteenth century. French, guessed Wilson. He thought the apartment was remarkably tasteful for a woman who looked like Jill Walsingham did at eleven thirty in the morning, and then guessed it was furnished. She crossed to a sideboard and turned off the radio. It was intrusive in the surroundings, an elaborate machine of dials and level meters and extension speakers.

They stood uncertainly in the centre of the room. Wilson said, 'I'd like to see you alone please, Mrs Walsingham.'

The woman looked to her husband. 'What's this about?'

'He's the director.'

'Alone please,' repeated Wilson.

'Why?' she said defiantly. The Australian accent was pronounced.

'I have some questions I'd like to ask you.'

'What about?'

Wilson looked pointedly at Walsingham, waiting for him to leave the room.

'Could we refuse?' she said.

'Of course.'

'What would happen if we did?'

'I'd suspend your husband from the embassy immediately and have you both taken back to London to answer the questions there.'

'What questions?'

Walsingham broke the impasse. 'I'm going to get myself a drink in the kitchen,' he said.

His wife's attitude softened almost immediately the door closed after him. 'What's he done?' she said.

'Has he done anything?'

'For Christ's sake!' she protested. 'When are you going to talk in a straight line?'

'From May 1969 until August of the same year you were a member of the Australian Communist party,' said Wilson.

She looked at him blank-faced.

'You were a member of the Communist party.'

'So what?'

'So your husband is a member of an intelligence department and there's no reference to your involvement on any records.'

'Because it wasn't a bloody involvement.' Her voice was a mixture of exasperation and incredulity.

'What was it then?'

'I was living with this fellow who thought the world was going the wrong way and wanted to get it right; he even had a beard, like Jesus. I was writing out posters saying Nixon and Kissinger were warmongers and he was screwing the girl who printed the newsletter.... In the cupboard where they kept the paper.'

'So you stopped?'

'Of course I stopped,' she said. 'Like I stopped believing that you catch a dose by sitting on dirty toilet seats.'

Wilson recognized the attempt to embarrass him was her way of fighting back. 'So there was no reason why it shouldn't have been listed on your husband's records?'

'No.'

'Why wasn't it?'

'How the hell do I know?'

'One of you does.'

She threw her arms out and her breasts wobbled, jelly-like. 'Ask him.'

'I did. He said he couldn't remember whether it was you or he who decided not to mention it.'

'We didn't talk about it.'

'I got the impression you did.'

'I don't remember it.'

'But you *gave* a reason for its not being mentioned,' said Wilson.

'You're twisting what I said.'

'No, I'm not.'

Jill Walsingham walked over to one of the antique chairs bordering the fireplace. Her attitude altered when she spoke again, the anger evaporating. 'Look,' she said, inviting belief. 'I suppose it must look bad, but it isn't. I don't know why Henry didn't put it down but there's nothing sinister in it. Honestly.'

'Who was the man?'

'What man?'

'The one you joined the Communist party to be with.'

143

'Ericson,' she said after a long pause. 'Stefan Ericson: his family were Swedish.'

'Do you maintain contact with him?'

'Of course not. I told you it was a schoolgirl thing that ended years ago.'

'And the party let you go, just like that?' Wilson snapped his fingers.

'I was only a probationary member anyway. People other than Stefan came around a few times but I told them to push off. In the end they stopped bothering.'

Wilson started towards the door but she stopped him. 'Sir Alistair.'

'Yes?'

'I'm sorry. For swearing and all that. I didn't mean to be rude.'

Wilson paused at the kitchen door, jerking it aside abruptly. Walsingham sat at a table by the sink, too far away to have overheard the conversation. There was a glass and a whisky bottle on the table beside him and the director thought it was early to be drinking.

'You can come back now,' he said.

'This is *my* home!' said Walsingham indignantly.

'And your job.' Without waiting for a response, Wilson returned to the room in which he had left Jill Walsingham. She had not moved from the chair.

When Walsingham entered, Wilson said, 'Your wife doesn't remember any discussion about omitting to mention the Communist affiliation. She thinks it must have been your decision.'

'It would have been something against me during annual review, wouldn't it?'

'Yes.'

'I'd hated being in the army and I'd hated working for my father in the City. But I loved security; I didn't want to lose that as well.'

'So you lied?'

'I didn't lie: I just didn't include it on the yearly paper.'

'A lie,' insisted Wilson. 'There's a specific question, about association with anything you consider might be subversive.'

144

'I didn't think of it as a lie.'

'Have you, at any time subsequent to 1969, been involved with anything you know or suspect might have been subversive?' Wilson was icily formal.

'No.'

'What about you, Mrs Walsingham?'

She responded slowly, as if she had been thinking of something else. 'Definitely not,' she said at last.

'This isn't serious, is it?' said Walsingham. 'I mean it won't affect the job or anything like that?'

'I'm not sure yet,' said the director.

For several moments after Wilson left neither of them spoke. Then Walsingham drove his fist into the palm of his other hand and said, 'Damn!'

'We knew it might happen.'

'Not after so long.'

'He'll get you, if he can.'

'Don't you think I hadn't realized that already!'

'There's no need to fight with me.'

'I'm sorry.'

'We've got to start being careful,' she said. 'Make sure nothing happens they can trick us with.'

'Yes,' he said.

'*Very* careful,' she said.

19

Inspector Moro's office was like the man, overflowing into untidiness. Against the far wall there was an ancient couch, leaking its horsehair stuffing through a collapsed sacking belly. The seat was confettied with papers that had dropped from the filing cabinets alongside. Moro's desk was in front of the only window in the room, fly-stained and unwashed behind venetian blinds. Papers were scattered over the desk and spilled, like a frozen waterfall, from a tiered set of plastic trays. There was a rust-spotted filing cabinet beneath framed diplomas made out in Moro's name. Nearly all the drawers were half open. On top was a potted geranium which had died in disgust. Charlie had accepted coffee, which came in a polystyrene cup; now he didn't know what to do with it.

'It's happening, just as we feared it would,' said Moro. 'The French have asked permission to send a contingent of their presidential security corps in addition to normal body-guards, and the Germans want to send an anti-terrorist squad as well.'

'Isn't that an over-reaction?' said Charlie. He'd suggested the meeting to convince the policeman of his intention to cooperate and reduce the possibility of Moro making inquiries about him in England. Being in a police station was not doing anything at all for his peace of mind.

'Of course it is,' said Moro. 'But because of it there had to be a cabinet meeting this morning. Afterwards there was an assurance to all Common Market governments that they would be adequately protected.... But it's still embarrassing.'

Charlie leaned forward and wedged his coffee cup onto

146

Moro's cluttered desk. The policeman appeared not to notice it was untouched.

'We agreed to cooperate,' said Charlie.

'So what have you to tell me?'

'Nothing,' said Charlie. Certainly not that he intended to try it alone if there were a sell-back approach rather than risk the interfering involvement of the police. That could ruin any handover and trap him in Italy until the Summit arrival of the intelligence protection.

'Then why are you here?'

'I thought it was two-way cooperation.'

Moro absentmindedly moved some papers on his desk. 'We've identified the blood group: it's AB negative.'

'It's a common group.'

'You got any police training?' said Moro suddenly.

Charlie's apprehension tightened several notches. He shook his head. 'Sort of thing you pick up over the years.'

'Common or not,' Moro said. 'It'll be the link when we get him.'

'You talked of fibres caught on the spikes.'

'Nylon,' said Moro. 'The sort of stuff used in men's jackets.'

'Have you traced the firm?'

'Only the manufacturers,' said Moro. 'They produce millions.'

'What about street informants: there must be a lot of talk over this.'

Moro gazed steadily at Charlie. 'That's the surprising thing,' he said. 'We're getting nothing back at all.'

The bastard still thinks I'm involved, thought Charlie. 'What about the servants at the villa?'

'All emphatic denials and good alibis.'

'And the embassy staff who had knowledge of security and the safe?'

'The only account we can't confirm is that of the security officer, Walsingham. He says his wife was at the cinema with a friend and he stayed all evening at his apartment. But there's no corroboration. Everyone's under surveillance.'

That was giving art a bad name, thought Charlie. 'It's still only twenty-four hours,' he said, unable to think of anything else.

'And you're still our best hope,' said Moro.

It had taken Igor Solomatin several weeks of patient searching to find an apartment suitable for their needs. Four separate houses had been modified and knocked together over the years, creating a labyrinthine collection of rooms and flats, on different levels and linked by sudden corridors. Its most obvious advantage were three separate entrances at the front and a spider's web of fire-escape grilles at the back. Vasily Leonov examined the empty, stale-smelling rooms with detached professionalism.

'How long will we be here?' he said.

'I'm allowing twenty minutes but I hope it will be over in fifteen,' said the Russian controller. 'The first is unimportant: we can take Fantani whenever we want. It's the second that matters. We've rehearsed the run over the distance and at the same time on five occasions and always arrived within three minutes of schedule. We expect the Englishman will do the same.'

'What's our escape margin?'

'Five minutes.'

'That's not long.'

'But sufficient.'

Solomatin depressed the button of a stop watch and led the way back out onto the main corridor. The stairway that provided the only access was almost directly opposite. Solomatin turned away to the left, where a doorway led into a corridor. 'It links with the next house,' said Solomatin. They halted on an adjoining landing. 'Down one flight and to the left is the rear fire escape.' Solomatin set off again at a leisurely pace, stopping the watch at the window leading out to the back of the building. 'Two minutes,' he said. 'Two more to get down. We'll be in the street before they come in the front door.'

'What if something goes wrong?' said Leonov. 'A breakdown? Or a puncture?'

'The whole purpose of sending him up and down the

autostrada is surveillance,' reminded Solomatin. 'We'll be with him all the time. The alarm won't be raised until he's reached the city and we can judge his arrival here to the minute.'

'There's still the chance of a mistake.' Leonov was unconvinced.

'Nothing will go wrong,' said Solomatin. 'In two days we'll be on our way back to Moscow to a hero's welcome.'

They left the building separately through different exits, and Solomatin drove across the city to Fantani's apartment in the Piazza del Popolo.

'I can move my fingers,' said the Italian, as Solomatin entered. 'It hurts but I can do it.'

'I told you it was only bruising.'

'Everything ready?'

Solomatin nodded. 'It's time to make the call.'

Charlie moved about the hotel room without direction, experiencing a loneliness he hadn't felt for a long time. He started opening and closing cupboards and doors. At the back of a shirt drawer was a pair of Clarissa's tights. For a moment he ran the material through his fingers, and then he dumped them in the waste bin. It was right that he should have told her to go. He just hadn't expected it to be like this.

Charlie sat on the edge of the bed, automatically removing his shoes and massaging his feet. He snatched out for the telephone when it rang, smiling in anticipation of her voice; then he recognized Billington.

'I've been given a meeting place,' said the ambassador. 'And instructions.'

'I didn't get the impression that the ambassador was particularly pleased,' said Naire-Hamilton. 'He said today was impossible so I've arranged it for tomorrow.'

'Does he know I'm with you?'

'Yes,' said the Permanent Under Secretary. 'What about Walsingham?'

'Circumstantially it looks strong.'

'Good enough to ship him home?'

'Possibly. But I'm going to leave him where he is. If he's the one, he'll panic to his control.'

'What if he doesn't?'

'We keep on looking.'

20

The surveillance was more inept than before. They used an unmarked police car again but it was away from the designated parking area – parked over yellow lines, showing it could ignore official restrictions. The same small man in the blue suit was in the passenger seat when Charlie passed. Pricks, he thought.

At the top of the Spanish Steps the Via Sistina balloons out and there is a taxi rank. Charlie asked for the Piazza Navona, because it was the first place that occurred to him. The police car pulled out to position itself with only one vehicle between them. The congestion that Charlie wanted began almost as soon as the taxi started down the Via della Mercede. At the junction with del Corso it became so heavy they had to stop completely. Charlie took a crumpled wad of lire from his pocket, looked at the meter and counted out double, to avoid any delaying argument. The taxi turned left onto del Corso. Traffic was freer, but there was still a tailback. The block was perfect: just beyond Tritone, with no side roads to allow the following driver to turn, Charlie gestured the taxi to the side of the road, and pressed the money into the driver's hand.

'I'll walk,' he said.

Charlie was back level with the police car before they properly realized what had happened. He walked smartly past, and from a window reflection in the Via del Tritone Charlie saw that the small man had got out and was actually running from the police car, which was still pointing in the wrong direction with the driver gesturing and shouting, in a vain attempt to clear a path for a U-turn.

Charlie's feet hurt, slowing him down. He stared about him for the right taxi arrangement. He let the first one go, because there was another close behind which the policeman could have taken. He was almost at the Crispi turning before he saw what he wanted, a vacant cab with only private vehicles behind. Charlie waited until it was practically level, then flagged it down. It was satisfying to watch the frustrated policeman run forward as if he half intended to stop the car, then gaze wildly around for a taxi of his own.

Charlie guessed Moro would trace the cab through the registration so he went all the way to the railway terminus rather than switch to another vehicle. He entered the station through one door, came out through another and picked up a third taxi which dropped him at the Borghese Gardens.

Traffic wasped around the piazza in front of him and Charlie decided against attempting to dodge his way through it. Instead he followed an old lady's example and used the crossing.

He liked Rome. It might be frayed at the edges, but it had style. Something that was missing from Harry's Bar. Charlie enjoyed beer in straight glasses in pubs without jukeboxes. Harry's Bar didn't have the jukeboxes, but it had pretensions that were deafening. It boasted chrome and mahogany and barmen who spoke eight languages. It was featured in all the guidebooks and a number of novels as the epitome of chic and was always crowded with people looking for the famous, who never came because people stood around looking for them.

Charlie made for the half-moon bar and saw that the stool stipulated for his identification was occupied. He ordered a whisky and took it to one of the minute tables against the wall. It was thirty minutes beyond the meeting time before Charlie was able to get the stool he wanted, reaching it a half-buttock ahead of a woman with a large hat and a poodle with a diamanté collar. She waited for Charlie to be gallant and then turned away tutting noisily. Charlie ordered another Scotch. With a better view of the bar, he tried to pick out his contact.

The woman with the poodle found a seat opposite him at

the far curve of the bar. She looked at Charlie with positive hostility. Charlie smiled. Up yours, he thought.

Charlie had expected the approach to come from the direction of the door or the lounge beyond, the most crowded part, but it didn't. He got an impression of someone behind him and turned to see the man at his left shoulder. The Gucci crest was on the shoes, belt and watch strap. The raw silk trousers were black and bum tight, worn with a shirt in contrasting white. It was silk and open at the neck, with several buttons undone to show a hairy chest cushioning a heavy gold medallion. A fawn jacket, worn the way that had always intrigued Charlie from those baffling Fellini films, was draped casually around his shoulders. But here there was a practical purpose: the jacket almost concealed a sling that supported a well-bandaged hand.

Seeing Charlie's look, the man said, 'It's inconvenient.'

'Particularly if a policeman sees it.'

The Italian shook his head. 'My fingerprints are on record, not palm impressions.' He was wiry and hard-bodied, with eyes that darted constantly. 'I burned the clothes, too,' he said. He nodded to the table. 'Let's sit away from the bar.'

Charlie followed, carrying his drink. If the man's finger-prints were on file, it wouldn't be hard to get a positive identification from criminal records when he went through the photographic files with Moro.

'I'm glad you came by yourself,' said the man. The English was accented but good. The cologne was very strong.

'You have the jewellery?' said Charlie.

'I might be able to arrange its return.'

Gangster-movie dialogue, thought Charlie. 'Good,' he said.

'There would be some expense.'

'How much?'

'Twenty-five per cent.'

'That's a lot.'

'Half a million is better for you than a full payout,' said the man.

153

'Yes,' said Charlie. 'It is.'

'Sterling, of course.'

'I want complete recovery.'

'How long will it take to arrange the finance?' asked the Italian.

'A day.'

'Tomorrow then?'

'Should be possible.'

'I'd like it to be tomorrow.'

Charlie intended to have the money numbered before he paid it over. That would make it useless and traceable. Moro could get his conviction. And Billington could recover his jewellery. Whether or not he made them available for any court exhibit would be a matter between him and the police. Willoughby wouldn't have any remaining liability. Better still, he wouldn't suffer any loss, because eventually the five hundred thousand would be returned. Everything would be tidied up nicely. Everything except Clarissa.

'Where shall we meet?' said Charlie.

'Further down this street at the corner of the Via Ludovisi there's a public telephone kiosk. Be there at noon. You'll be called and told what to do.'

'I'll be there,' said Charlie.

'Be by yourself. You'll be watched all the time. If there's any sign of a policeman, it's off.'

'I'll be alone,' said Charlie.

'Until tomorrow then.' The Italian shrugged the jacket closer around his shoulders to keep the sling under cover and made an elegant exit from the bar. Probably danced a hell of a tango, thought Charlie. He didn't hurry to leave, holding the glass before him in both hands and staring down into the amber liquid. Everything had gone according to plan. But it just didn't feel right. It was a nagging, persistent uncertainty, like a stone in his shoe. Unable to resolve it, he beckoned the barman, paid and left the bar.

Outside, the street was thick with people, cars and noise. Charlie threaded his way down the Via Veneto, marking the telephone that had been identified. Moro would have reacted to his evasion by now and would be concentrating upon the hotel as the only known contact point. So he couldn't go back immediately. Charlie chose a post office with an overseas telephone section. There was no line congestion, so Charlie was connected at once. Willoughby's anxiety was obvious.

'Thank God,' he said.

'Keep praying until I've bought it back,' said Charlie.

'How much?'

'Five hundred thousand. In sterling.'

Willoughby's sigh of relief was audible.

'Is that going to be possible?' Charlie decided against telling the underwriter how he intended to recover the buy-back money.

'Just about,' said Willoughby. 'I'm indebted to you, Charlie. Where do you want it sent?'

'The main Bank of Rome.'

'It should be there first thing tomorrow.'

Which would give him sufficient time to record the numbers.

'Charlie,' blurted the underwriter.

'What?'

'I'm sorry.'

'What for?'

'Just sorry,' said Willoughby, breaking the connection.

Charlie queued patiently to pay for the call. If there were an apology, it should have been his to the underwriter, he thought.

As he walked back to the Grand Ville up the gently sloping streets, Charlie determined to keep Walsingham out of it at this stage, wanting to restrict his contact with the embassy to the minimum. About fifty yards from the hotel, Charlie saw the car with the boot antennae move and knew they'd seen him. It accelerated too fast and stopped too quickly, so there was a screech of brakes and people turned.

The man in the blue suit had the door open before the car stopped.

'Get in,' he said. His shoes were still stained with horse piss.

Inspector Moro was quite calm, which increased the sense of

menace. He lounged back from the crowded desk, eyes fixed on the ceiling and talking in a consciously controlled voice. His jacket was rucked up from his shoulders, heightening the skin-shedding appearance.

'I warned you,' he said. 'I warned you and you ignored me.'

'I didn't.'

'You dodged from a taxi in the Via del Corso to another that took you to the railway terminal,' said Moro. 'There you immediately got into a third car which took you to the top of the Via Veneto. We traced you that far.'

'I'd have been disappointed if you hadn't.'

The reply seemed to confuse the inspector. 'I told you there were to be no arrangements without my being involved. You ignored me. Who did you meet?'

'No one.'

'Don't treat me like a fool.' Moro's voice rose for the first time.

'Don't treat me like a criminal.'

'What!'

'I agreed to do nothing without telling you first,' said Charlie. 'It was an undertaking I intended to keep. Having given my word, I don't expect to be pursued everywhere I go.'

'Are you saying you evaded my people as some sort of stupid protest?'

'Yes,' said Charlie. 'And to prove their ineffectiveness.' It didn't sound as good as he'd hoped it would; in fact it sounded bloody awful.

'*I* decide how to run an investigation: whether or not to impose surveillance,' said Moro.

'If you weren't going to trust me there was little purpose in our agreeing to an arrangement in the first place.'

The policeman had not expected attack and was finding it difficult to adjust. 'I meant it,' he said. 'About what I would do if you tried anything independently.'

'I never doubted you for a second.' Now was the moment to change his mind, to admit everything and go with Moro through the records until they got a name. If he did that, the entrapment would never work; not the sort the police would attempt. Charlie said nothing.

'Did you have a meeting with anyone today?' repeated the policeman.

'No.' Now he was committed.

'If I find that to be a lie, then you're guilty of impeding a police investigation.'

'I know that.'

'I want to know anything, the moment it happens,' said Moro.

'You said that before,' reminded Charlie.

'This time, believe me.'

Sir Alistair Wilson replaced the telephone after Harkness's London call and turned back into the communal suite towards Naire-Hamilton and Jackson.

'That's interesting,' he said.

'What is?' demanded the Permanent Under Secretary.

'Richard Semingford has written to Foreign Office personnel asking about pension entitlement and the size of the sum that's commutable in the event of his leaving.'

21

Italian banks open at eight thirty in the morning. Charlie was ready early, wanting as much time as possible to list the currency numbers. Today there was no vehicle with the familiar aerial. As he walked by the Medici Hotel, a man who had been studying the tariff pushed slightly too quickly through the swing doors and Charlie smiled at the hurried avoidance. He was curious to see how they'd follow his taxi. The mobile cover was better. They'd positioned cars at intervals along the street, so that the contact would be taken up not with a vehicle pulling out in obvious pursuit but emerging first in front and then letting the taxi overtake. It was the black Lancia, decided Charlie. The driver wore a cap, as if he were the chauffeur, and the observer rode in the back reading a newspaper, but holding it in such a way that his view of the taxi wasn't obscured. Charlie knew there wouldn't be any second chance, if anything went wrong.

At the Bank of Rome an assistant manager took him to a deputy manager and the deputy manager took him to the manager. Charlie produced his accreditation from Rupert Willoughby and the manager confirmed that the money draft had been received the previous night. Charlie stipulated cash rather than a letter of credit and asked for the numbers to be run through a computer for record. The manager allowed a brief expression of irritation and summoned back the deputy manager. Together they went to the basement and the notes were distributed between two programmers. It took two hours to complete the list. Charlie ascended to the manager's office, calculating that by now Moro would have the exterior of the building under siege.

'Thank you for your assistance,' said Charlie.

Believing Charlie wanted the numbers recorded against loss, the manager said, 'A letter of credit would have been simpler.'

'I'm afraid my client insists upon cash.'

'Of course,' said the manager, eager to terminate the meeting.

'But I accept the danger,' said Charlie. 'I wonder if I can impose upon you a little more?'

The manager frowned.

'This is a large sum of money,' said Charlie, hefting the case as if the man needed proof. 'Despite the precaution with the listing, I'm still nervous of carrying it unguarded.'

'You want a security guard?'

'A security van,' said Charlie. 'It's a comparatively short distance; little more than three or four kilometres.'

'I suppose that can be arranged,' said the manager reluctantly.

It was the turn of the deputy manager to escort Charlie through the rear of the building into a completely enclosed yard. There was a burst of hurried Italian and Charlie saw one of the drivers grimace at the interruption to his routine. The armoured, grilled vehicle had no windows at the rear doors and only a small barred aperture, with a microphone to communicate with the driver. Charlie climbed in and smiled his thanks.

It took less than five minutes to reach the Via Ludovisi, and Charlie was beside the box ten minutes early. From the same pavement table at Doney's where he had identified the Italian to Leonov three evenings before, Igor Solomatin sipped an espresso and watched. With a minute to go before the arranged time, he raised the copy of *Il Messagero*, giving the signal to Fantani inside.

To ensure the line had not become blocked, Charlie had entered the kiosk at five to twelve, going through an elaborate performance of consulting dialling-code instructions. The telephone rang promptly at noon.

'Very good,' said the voice he recognized from the previous day. 'You're alone.'

'I said I would be,' reminded Charlie. 'Do you have what I want?'

'Do you?'

'Can't you see the case?'

'I don't know what's inside.'

'It's all there,' said Charlie.

'You'll need a car. To your right is an Avis sign. Once you've hired the car, go north out of the city. The autostrada to Milan is numbered A1. Almost as soon as you join, there's an Agip gas station. Ignore it. Drive on for about fifty kilometres. There is a slip road to your right. Just after the indicator sign is another Agip station. Stop there.'

'Then what?'

'Go into the station shop. Be by the telephone there at four.'

Another entrapment precaution. 'Aren't we letting this drag on?' said Charlie.

The response was immediate. 'We don't want anything to go wrong, do we?'

A man trained in diplomacy can convey offence as well as avoid it. Billington conveyed it extremely well. He came stiffly forward to meet them, the handshakes a passing formality. He ignored the desk area, leading the director and Naire-Hamilton to part of the embassy office furnished with leather, club-like chairs. Before they sat he said, 'I consider you have been extremely discourteous.'

Wilson and Naire-Hamilton remained standing. 'That wasn't our intention,' said Wilson.

The ambassador's face was flushed. 'There is protocol,' he said. 'If you wished to question one of my staff, then I should have been informed in advance.'

'An unfortunate oversight,' said Naire-Hamilton.

Belatedly Billington indicated chairs and they sat. 'Is there anything wrong with Walsingham?' he said.

'His wife had some Communist contact, when she was a student in Australia,' said Wilson.

'In the thirties flirting with Communism was a popular pastime.' Billington's sarcasm was pointed.

'This was in 1969,' said Wilson. 'And he didn't declare it on his personnel records.'

'I should have hardly thought this justified your coming all the way from London,' said Billington.

'There's also the Summit,' said Naire-Hamilton.

A secretary arrived with coffee. She put it on a table between them and poured. No one spoke until she left the room.

'I understood you'd already sent people to look after that,' said the ambassador. 'They've been here for days.'

'That was before the robbery,' said Wilson.

'What's the robbery got to do with it?'

'I thought you might be able to tell me.'

Billington edged forward on his seat. 'You're being obtuse.'

'Was anything more than jewellery taken?'

'I beg your pardon!' Billington's face was getting redder.

'Work sometimes gets taken home; records show that various members of the embassy travel quite regularly to Ostia. It's slightly unusual for an ambassador to spend so much time away from the official residence.'

'Nothing leaves the security vault which isn't cleared to do so,' said Billington. 'I resent the implication of it even being considered. There was not nor has there ever been any authorized documentation kept in my personal safe. It would have been a direct contravention of all security regulations, as you are perfectly well aware.'

'I'm glad of the reassurance,' said Wilson. 'You appreciate, surely, that the inquiry had to be made?'

'No, I do not,' said Billington. 'And I intend to protest most strongly to the Foreign Office about both the manner and implication of this visit.'

As they walked back along the wide corridor towards the main exit, Naire-Hamilton said, 'What on earth was the point in behaving like that?'

'There's no security classification on a complaint,' said the director. 'Within half an hour of it being sent, there won't be anyone in the embassy unaware of our presence. If it isn't Walsingham we've got to cause someone else to panic.'

Fantani had emerged from Doney's by the time Charlie completed the hiring formalities and took a seat beside the Russian. Fantani strained to identify the car, but the rental office was too far away and he gave up.

'My people know what they're doing,' said Solomatin. 'He'll be covered all the way. And back.'

'It all seems very complicated.' Fantani gently attempted finger exercises with his damaged hand.

'We've got to be absolutely sure there's no police involvement,' said Solomatin.

'I make the next call from the Via Salaria?' said Fantani.

Solomatin counted out some coins to pay for his coffee, feeling a reluctance to take the man there. It was the first time he had been so closely involved with violence and he was nervous. 'We'd better go,' he said.

22

He was having to wave his arms and legs when the strings were pulled, and Charlie Muffin had never liked the puppet's role: he preferred to be the one in control, the manipulator. He took the car angrily from the link road onto the autostrada, careless of the blare of protest from a Fiat on the inside lane. Charlie knew he was going to get a lot of pleasure screwing that shifty-eyed little sod.

For several kilometres he concentrated upon the cars travelling around him at the same speed, then without warning pulled over onto the hard shoulder. There was another screech of horns from behind but Charlie ignored it. He got out of the hire car and kicked the front offside tyre, as if to check a possible puncture. Appearing satisfied, he got back in, waited for a gap in the traffic and rejoined the motorway. Charlie was confident he would have been too quick for any following vehicle to avoid passing him, so he drove looking for any familiar car that might be waiting ahead for him to catch up. He clocked ten kilometres and detected nothing. Bugger them, he thought.

Charlie saw the service station ahead, indicated and turned smoothly into the forecourt. He was thirty minutes early, so he topped up the petrol and moved the car away from the pumps into the parking area. It was a busy station, cars and lorries and people swirling around. Well chosen, thought Charlie: greater professionalism than he would have expected, in fact.

He found the telephone in the vending area and went to it, the card Walsingham had given him ready in his hand. The security man came curtly on the line, the eagerness obvious in his voice.

'Something up?'

'There might be,' said Charlie. 'I just wanted to know where I could contact you later.'

'I'm leaving the embassy now.'

'Where to?'

'Home. You've got the number. We're going to be there all night.'

'Stay there,' said Charlie.

'Where are you?'

'Miles up some bloody autostrada,' said Charlie. 'They're making sure I haven't got the police with me.'

'Shall I tell the ambassador?'

'Not yet,' said Charlie. 'If there's no contact here, it'll be a waste of time.' There was always the possibility that Moro would contact the embassy once he knew he'd been tricked at the bank.

'What do you want me to do?'

'Just wait.'

'Sure I can't help any more than that?'

'Not yet.'

'It's not much.'

'It will be, when the time comes.'

Charlie replaced the receiver and lingered in the sales area, always keeping the clock in sight. Christ, time was going slowly. He checked his watch to ensure the station clock hadn't stopped and then pushed his hands into his pockets, annoyed at his nervousness. Right to be tense, before a thing like this. But not nervous: nervous people made mistakes. The stone-in-the-shoe feeling came again. He couldn't have missed anything; there was nothing to miss. It was a straightforward robbery with a straightforward settlement.

He went to the kiosk early, once more to keep the line clear, lifting the telephone at the first ring.

'You're doing very well,' said the voice.

Wait, you bastard; just wait, thought Charlie. 'Are we going to do it here?' he said.

'No.'

'Where?'

'Back in Rome.'

'Fuck me!'

There was a moment's silence. Then the instructions continued uninterrupted. 'Come back into Rome. Find your way to the Via Salaria. From 19 to 45 there's an apartment complex. You need 35. Use the centre doorway. It's facing you on the third floor, at the top of the stairs.'

It was a bloody awful set-up but he didn't have a choice, Charlie realized. 'I've got it,' he said. 'What time?'

'It'll take you an hour to get back to Rome. We'll allow fifteen minutes for unforeseen delay. Be there at eight fifteen.'

'All right.'

'Arrive alone,' said the voice. 'If you don't, there'll be no one in the apartment when you get there.'

'I understand,' said Charlie. When Moro staged the identity parade he'd pretend to walk by at first, so the smart little bugger would think he'd got away with it.

'Don't be late.' The line went dead.

Charlie dialled again. At the first attempt Charlie got a woman who identified herself as Walsingham's wife and said he had not yet returned from the embassy. Charlie wandered impatiently around the service area, letting five minutes pass on the slow-moving clock. The security man answered the second time.

'I've got a meeting place,' announced Charlie.

'Genuine?'

'How do I know?'

'Do you want me to come?'

Charlie calculated thirty minutes for the transfer. 'Make it eight forty-five,' he said.

'Where?'

'35 Via Salaria: centre door. I'll be waiting.'

'What about the ambassador?'

Charlie hesitated. Get the jewellery back to Billington first and then advise Moro. 'Tell him,' he said.

'What about the police?'

'I'll do that, when it's over; it could all still be a hoax.'

'You don't really believe that, do you?'

'I'd be wasting everybody's bloody time, if I did.'

'Good luck.'

'Yeah,' said Charlie.

In his apartment overlooking the Tiber, Walsingham put down the telephone and his wife said, 'Did you get it?'

'Of course I got it,' said Walsingham.

'You going to tell the ambassador?'

'Yes.'

'Watch your back,' she said. 'Just don't forget to watch your back. They're bastards, all of them. Rotten capitalist bastards.'

The inquiries had been made overnight and, because of the time difference with Australia, the reply from Canberra arrived almost at the same time as confirmation of Walsingham's salary from London. The information had no outside relevance and Harkness telephoned direct to the Eden, relaying the details to Jackson.

'After stoppages, Walsingham's salary is seven hundred and eighty pounds a month,' said Jackson to Naire-Hamilton and the director.

'The apartment rental is five hundred and sixty-five,' reminded Wilson.

'Which only leaves two hundred and fifty.' Jackson checked the London information. 'There's a housing allowance of a hundred pounds,' he added.

'Still an expensive choice,' said Naire-Hamilton. 'What about Australia?'

'Stefan Ericson is still a political activist,' read out Jackson. 'He remembers Jill Walsingham, or rather Littleton, as she was then.'

'What about her?'

'He says she was quite politically aware.'

'Why did she quit after only three months?'

'Nothing to do with her politics, according to Ericson: it was over some row they had, because he became involved with another woman. Jill didn't want to continue their relationship.'

The telephone sounded again and Jackson answered it. 'The ambassador,' he said to Wilson.

The director took the phone.

'Is Walsingham suspect?' asked Billington at once.

'Why?'

'I think I've been rather indiscreet.' There was an obvious reluctance in Billington's admission.

'What do you mean?'

'I've allowed myself to be persuaded that the jewellery stolen from Ostia could be recovered by some sort of ransom. I appointed Walsingham to act as a liaison between me and the insurance assessor.'

'So?'

'Walsingham has just telephoned. He's off to see the man Muffin this evening.'

For several moments Wilson remained silent, the telephone held slightly away from his head. 'What!' he demanded. The others in the room were aware of the sudden rigidity of his body.

'I said Walsingham was going to.... '

'... *No!*' shouted the director. 'The name. What was the name you used?'

'Muffin,' said the ambassador. 'Charles Muffin. He is an insurance assessor from London.'

'I thought there were going to be others here for protection,' said Fantani. The nervousness had grown since the conversation with Charlie Muffin on the autostrada. He was moving restlessly around the room, eyes darting about him.

'For the handover,' said Solomatin. 'Any minute now.'

'It'll be all right, won't it?' said Fantani. 'I mean I gave the instructions properly?'

'Fine,' assured Solomatin. 'You were just fine.'

When he heard a soft knock at the door, the Italian smiled and said, 'Your people?'

'Yes,' said Solomatin. He opened it and Vasily Leonov came quickly in off the corridor.

'Sorry, I can't shake hands,' said Fantani, indicating his tightly strapped arm.

Leonov, who couldn't speak Italian and didn't understand the remark, raised his hand anyway and Fantani had the briefest glimpse of the Tokarev before it fired. He was killed instantly, his body lifted back over the chair arm and then folding sideways, so that he ended in an oddly crouched position, as if he were praying.

Behind, Solomatin retched. Leonov turned to him curiously and said, 'What's the matter?'

On the other side of town Henry Walsingham replaced the receiver after the telephone call and said, 'They've changed the time: it's eight o'clock.'

23

The photograph that Sir Alistair Wilson had ordered from London had arrived by the time he and Naire-Hamilton got to the embassy. They went directly to the communications room, unpeeling it from the transmission drum, and carried it limply into the ambassador's office. Billington's antipathy still showed. The intelligence chief decided to ignore it. He thrust the picture towards the ambassador and said, 'Is this the man?'

'Yes,' he said. 'Why?'

Wilson's whole body appeared to deflate. 'He's a traitor,' he said simply. 'Seven years ago he wrecked an intelligence department.'

Billington laughed uncertainly. 'You can't be serious!'

'I wish I weren't.'

'Good God!'

'I want to know everything,' said Wilson.

'There's little to tell. I warned my underwriter I wanted the jewellery revalued, according to the policy terms and they sent this man. He spent two days at the villa, checking the security and itemizing the pieces. Then he came on the day of the robbery and told me the thieves would most likely offer it back, at a price. And asked me to cooperate....'

'What happened tonight?' demanded the intelligence director.

'I had a call from Walsingham about an hour ago. He said Muffin had contacted him and that an exchange had been agreed. He was meeting him and hoped to recover the jewellery.'

From the surveillance already imposed, Wilson knew the

security man was still in his apartment. And there were five men outside, waiting to follow wherever he went.

'Did he say where the meeting was taking place?'

'Some apartment complex on the Via Salaria.... 35, I think. Yes, 35.'

'What time?'

'Eight forty-five.'

Wilson and Naire-Hamilton looked at their watches simultaneously. 'Still more than an hour,' said the Permanent Under Secretary.

'We're going to get him!' said Wilson in a sudden flare of confidence.

'What about the police?' suggested the ambassador.

'No!' It was Naire-Hamilton who spoke, his voice loud. Seeming surprised at his own outburst he said more quietly. 'Not yet.'

'We're risking an incident,' said Billington.

'We're attempting to avoid one,' said Naire-Hamilton.

'I have ultimate responsibility here,' said the ambassador.

'It's a debatable point,' said Naire-Hamilton. 'If you want a ruling I suggest you contact the Prime Minister's office.'

'Would someone tell me what's going on?' demanded Billington.

Henry Walsingham let his car coast slowly along the Via Salaria as he strained through the darkness to make out the numbering. The rush-hour traffic was still heavy and there were hoots of irritation from behind him. The security man parked and checked the time, relieved that he was five minutes early. He felt like he had during the army exercises, particularly on the plains of Germany, with men behind him and hoping to Christ he didn't make a ridiculous mistake.

He got out, unaware of the two following cars that had stopped a hundred yards away. For a moment Walsingham stared up at the jagged rooftops outlined against the night sky and then pushed through the centre door as instructed. He found the pushlight which dimly illuminated the stairs curling away from him. There was no lift. Walsingham climbed steadily, pausing on the first and second landings for the light switch.

Number 35 faced him, as he came puffing to the third floor. He listened at the door for voices and heard nothing. His first knock was hesitant. There was no reply. He rapped again more forcefully.

Solomatin opened the door and said in Italian, 'I'm glad you're not late: come in.'

As Walsingham stepped forward, Leonov crossed the landing from the linking corridor entrance opposite. There was a shot no louder than the heavy closing of a door. The impact forced Walsingham across the room, arms outstretched. His body slid when it hit the floor so that one hand was almost touching Fantani's.

'Go on!' said Leonov urgently.

Solomatin knelt down and edged a key into Walsingham's pocket, pulling hurriedly back as soon as he had done it. Leonov tossed the gun down beside the body, and followed Solomatin out. They were through into the adjoining building and making for the rear fire escape when Wilson's car stopped behind the observer team already in position.

24

Sir Alistair Wilson deferred to Jackson's experience as a field operator. During the short drive from the embassy he briefed the supervisor and then held back while Jackson organized the surveillance teams. The director's car, which was being used for control, was moved from the Via Salaria to a cul-de-sac opposite. Jackson reversed the vehicle into it and extinguished the lights.

'How long?' he asked the director.

'Twenty minutes, according to Walsingham.'

Jackson quickly left the car, crossing to the apartment block and paced out a distance, checking to see if their vehicles were conspicuous. He dodged back between the traffic and sat heavily into the driving seat. 'Good enough,' he said.

'Everybody understands?'

'Perfectly. They're to let him go in and then seal the place.'

The director stared across at the building. 'Looks like a warren.'

'Well chosen.'

Wilson grunted.

'What happens if he doesn't show up on time?'

'We give it fifteen minutes,' he said. 'And then go in.'

'What do you think he's doing here?'

'Whatever it is, he's the key. He's got to be.'

Along the main highway in front of them traffic fireflied by in a continuous flicker of lights. In the cul-de-sac vehicles were parked in careless Rome fashion, half on and half off the pavement. There were bicycles secured to railings by chains.

'How much damage did he really do?'

'A lot,' said Wilson. 'The CIA director, as well as our own controller, was seized, for exchange with a spy of their own. It's taken years to build up confidence with Washington again. Kalenin was supposed to be crossing into Vienna: the Americans had put in almost a hundred people on the ground and we matched them, man for man. It was obviously impractical to take them all back into Czechoslovakia. The Russians fingerprinted and photographed the bloody lot of them.'

'Bastard.'

Wilson looked apprehensively to the man beside him. 'I don't want him hurt,' he said. 'Not until I can gauge the extent of the damage.'

'We'll wait,' said Jackson.

Wilson tensed as the car stopped opposite but relaxed as a young couple got out, laughing and hugging. He massaged the joint of his stiffened leg. It wasn't cold so there was no reason for it to ache.

Conscious of the movement, Jackson said from beside him. 'Waiting always screws me up.'

'We've been waiting a long time for this one,' said Wilson.

Charlie had become engulfed in the rush hour on the outskirts of the city, stop-starting his way through the congestion. Impatiently he had tried short cuts, guessing the general direction, and become blocked by even worse jams. He'd fought against the irritation, knowing it was pointless, and submitted at last to the slow crawl.

It was seven thirty before he approached the centre of Rome and three stops before he found someone with sufficient English to explain the route. But once in the Via Salaria Charlie had little problem finding the number.

It was bad. Unprotected and carrying half a million pounds, he was having to walk into a bloody great building in which a hundred villains could be hiding, just waiting for his head to emerge around a stairwell. In the old days he'd have had twenty men already moving through the building disguised as cleaners, janitors and repair men. And another squad outside, for additional protection. Charlie scratched his nose. He'd buggered it up and the old days were gone for ever. He considered taking a tyre lever from the boot but quickly dismissed it; if there were to be an ambush, a tyre lever would be about as effective as spitting at a house fire.

Charlie checked the mirror until the traffic eased and then got out of the car, pulling the case behind him. Instinctively he looked both ways along the road, squinting to see into the parked vehicles; it looked safe enough, but in a place like this it was impossible to be sure without back-up.

The middle door, he remembered. He pushed gently against it, feeling it give at once beneath the pressure, and eased through into the darkness. He barked his knuckles against the time switch but was grateful for the light. Somewhere in the distance he heard a baby's cry, long and protracted. Charlie realized he was sweating, the handle of the case slippery beneath his fingers. The light clicked off before he reached the first landing, so that he had to make the last few steps in darkness.

The baby's cry was louder and he wondered why somebody didn't do anything about it: the Italians were supposed to love kids. He found the switch again and continued cautiously upwards. Somewhere above a door opened and closed and he waited for footsteps but none came. The second landing was as empty as the first. Charlie lighted the way but didn't begin the final climb. He put the case between his feet and wiped his hands along the sides of his trousers. The baby had stopped crying; he hadn't been aware of its happening. There wasn't a sound now in the whole building. Only Charlie's laboured breathing. He saw the apartment the moment he pressed the third-floor switch. The door was ajar. He went past 35 and found the link corridor into the next building; it was deserted. He came back to the door, listening against it. And then pushed it wider, not attempting to enter. He saw Walsingham's body first, on his face and spreadeagled, and then the hand of someone else.

Every nerve, every instinct, every memory of his basic training, screamed at Charlie not to go in. He did.

The Italian was staring glazed-eyed at the ceiling: there was a lot of blood on his chest where the artery had burst, and it was difficult to see the exact wound.

Charlie noticed a Gucci bag near a side table and was stretching towards it when he saw the gun, partially concealed beneath Walsingham's body. He recognized it at once as a Russian weapon. There was a second of numbed shock then a voice behind him shouted, 'Stay where you are!'

There were three men just inside the door, fanned out so they had him in a twenty-five-degree arc of crossfire. They were hunched in standard marksman position, legs bent, pistol arm fully extended, the other hand clamped to the wrist to minimize the recoil.

Behind the gunmen was an elderly, wisp-haired man. He said, 'Any move, no matter how slight, and they'll fire. Not to kill you; it'll be into your legs, to cripple you.'

He waited, appearing to expect a response. Then he said, 'We've got you, Charlie Muffin.'

The ambassador and Naire-Hamilton listened grave-faced for the intelligence director to finish the explanation and then Naire-Hamilton said, 'It's a nasty one. Very nasty indeed.'

'What are we going to do?' demanded Billington.

'Recover as best we can,' suggested the Permanent Under Secretary. To the ambassador he said, 'I think you'd better contact the Italian government right away.'

25

The preparations had begun before their arrival, but men were still working when Charlie was led down the stairs into the main storeroom of the embassy basement. An area about twenty feet square had been cleared, the boxes and containers pushed against the far wall and stacked into a floor-to-ceiling barrier. Charlie expected the questioning to start at once, but he was pushed into an annex, below ground and without any windows. Against the far wall there was a cot with one blanket, and beside it a bucket to pee in. Henry Jackson followed Charlie into the cell and snapped his fingers.

'Let's have them,' he said.

Charlie thought, fleetingly, of feigning ignorance but then dismissed it as pointless; everything would be pointless from now on. He bent, extracting the laces from his shoes, and handed them to the man, together with his tie and belt. Jackson pointed towards the bed and said, 'Everything in your pockets on there.'

Methodically Charlie began unloading. There was a comb in his top pocket, passport and travellers' cheques inside his jacket, his airline ticket with the baggage label still attached, a crumpled sponge of Italian paper money, a pen, the keys to the Battersea apartment, a driving licence and one neatly folded square of toilet paper.

'Linings.'

Dutifully Charlie turned all the pockets inside out. He stood in front of the man, clutching his trousers and aware of the barely subdued hostility.

'Watch.'

Charlie unstrapped it from his wrist.

'Know what I'd like to do?' said Jackson.

'What?'

'I'd like to kick the shit out of you.'

Charlie had been waiting for the beating. He tightened his body against the attack and the man sniggered.

'The name's Jackson,' he said. 'Remember it. I'm going to be the first.'

He scooped Charlie's belongings into a plastic envelope and closed the door. There was only the sound of a single lock and Charlie didn't think the woodwork looked particularly resistant. He dismissed the speculation as academic. He was not going anywhere any more.

The seizure at the apartment house and the bundled drive, with his hands manacled painfully behind him, had been too hurried for him to examine his situation with any detachment. But, alone in his rectangular box smelling of decayed, abandoned paper, Charlie confronted the realization that, after seven years of middle-of-the-night wakefulness and gut-heaving at casual glances, they'd got him. An overwhelming feeling of helplessness settled over him. The muscles in his thighs began jerking in involuntary spasms and he sat down quickly upon the cot, wrapping his arms around his legs. The man ... what was his name? Jackson ... Jackson had said there'd be a beating. Why not at once? Maybe the standard technique, complete solitude, to let the fear seep in, and make sure there was no sleep to complete the disorientation. Scalpalomine maybe. But why? That was standard procedure to break someone, to erode a false cover or deceit. They knew who he was. And what he'd done. He didn't have a cover story to destroy: he had no one to protect.

Charlie rolled sideways onto the bed, keeping his knees in a foetal ball under his chin. He didn't want anything to happen to Willoughby. Clarissa either. Particularly Clarissa. He tried to put her from his mind and concentrate on his surroundings. Was this what he could expect from now on? An eight foot by twelve existence, with a cot and a bucket, and water dripping down the walls?

From outside came the sound of heavy things being shifted

and scraped across the floor; twice there were footsteps seemingly right outside and Charlie raised his head apprehensively. Both times they receded. He looked at his wrist, before remembering the watch had gone. A time check was one of the first things to establish, according to the resistance technique: something else he'd forgotten. An hour, Charlie estimated: maybe longer. He closed his eyes against the light. *'Trust me, Edith. We'll beat the bastards'*. He hadn't. Not in the end.

Charlie reckoned it was another hour before they came for him. He managed to swing his legs to the floor before they reached him. There was another man with Jackson. Charlie blinked at them, gritty-eyed even though he hadn't slept.

'Up,' said Jackson.

Charlie rose, grasping at his waistband. The Hush Puppies threatened to fall off and he had to scuff his feet across the floor. The only obvious change in the room beyond was a baize-topped table, positioned near the centre. There was a smaller table alongside and as he got closer Charlie noticed the tape recorder. From a more darkened part of the basement a man came into the light and sat behind the machine. He didn't bother to look up.

'Sit down,' said Wilson. He was seated in the centre of the table, clearly the questioner. Naire-Hamilton was to his left.

Charlie sat.

The operator started the tape.

'Your name is Charles Muffin?' said Wilson.

'Yes,' said Charlie. It had been a long time since he'd heard his Christian name properly.

'You were for eighteen years a Grade 1 operative within the security service of Great Britain?'

'Yes.' Had it really been as long as that?

'And as such signed an undertaking governed by the Official Secrets Act?'

'Yes.' Charlie coughed, not wanting his voice to betray any nervousness when he was called upon to respond in any greater detail.

'Did you at some date in 1977, communicate with the Soviet Union?'

It seemed so damning, put as bluntly as that. 'Yes,' said Charlie.

'How?' demanded Wilson.

'Through Vienna. I made contact with the Soviet embassy.' His voice remained controlled.

'With whom?'

'A KGB colonel.'

'What was his name?'

'Valery Kalenin.'

'Did you know of this man?'

'I knew he was operational head of the Komitet Gosudarst-vennoy Bezpasnosti.'

'What was the purpose of the meeting?'

Revenge. To teach arrogant bastards they couldn't throw him to the dogs, like so much disposable meat. But whichever way he attempted to put it, the explanation would make him what they'd already decided, a traitor. 'Nine months earlier I had controlled the arrest of a man running a Soviet spy cell in Britain. His name was Alexei Berenkov. During the final stages of that operation we needed documents from East Berlin proving the man's identity to be Russian. To create a diversion and minimize the risk of the documents being intercepted, the department arranged for my capture. The car they had marked as the one I should have been driving was destroyed. Had I been in it, I would have died.' Charlie licked his lips. Not bad so far, he thought. 'I suspected a set-up. An East German who believed I was arranging his crossing into West Berlin drove the car; I returned by U-bahn. The purpose of the Vienna meeting was retribution, against people who had decided I was expendable.' A bad finish, conceded Charlie.

'Retribution?' said Wilson.

'The Soviet Union never allows captured spies to endure long imprisonment. They wanted an exchange and I provided people for it.'

'Who?'

'The British and American directors. Kalenin let it be understood he wanted to cross to the West. Both directors went to Austria to receive him. They were taken by Soviet commandos to be held until there was a swap.'

'You knowingly betrayed to a hostile power the identity and whereabouts of the two most senior officials?' said Wilson.

'An exchange was guaranteed: that was the only reason for their seizure. I knew they wouldn't be held for more than two or three weeks.' In a barren room surrounded by impassive men, it sounded a weak plea of mitigation.

'At the end of 1977, after the seizure of your superior officers, you defected to the Soviet Union?' said Wilson. Charlie stared blankly across the small table at the director.

'We got your London address from your driving documents,' said Wilson. 'I've had the place entered: we found everything.'

'I don't know what you're talking about,' said Charlie. It sounded fatuous, he realized.

'We know you have killed three British agents during the last ten months. And about your connection with Walsingham.'

'No!' Charlie stiffened and instantly felt hands on both his shoulders, forcing him back into his chair. 'I admit what I did in Vienna,' he said. 'I don't understand anything else you're saying.'

The asthma banded around his chest, squeezing the breath from his lungs.

It was midnight when the director and the Permanent Under Secretary got to Billington's office.

'The Italians are furious,' said the ambassador. 'I've been officially summoned to the Foreign Ministry tomorrow. They want a full explanation.'

'We'd rather it wasn't given,' said Naire-Hamilton.

'That's preposterous,' said Billington. 'You've trampled all over the scene of a killing, removed bodies and evidence and disregarded absolutely that any Italian sovereignty exists.'

'It was necessary,' insisted Naire-Hamilton.

'They'll never accept that.'

'Ask them to expand the meeting tomorrow,' suggested Wilson. 'Include their security people. And promise our attendance.'

'You?' The ambassador appeared surprised.

'It would be easier than briefing you,' said Wilson. 'We don't think the Italians will want a scandal so near the Summit. Any more than we do.'

'You can't conceal crime,' protested Billington.

'When it's necessary you can,' said Naire-Hamilton easily.

Trying to force a little calm, Billington looked towards a drinks tray and said, 'Would you like anything?'

Both Wilson and Naire-Hamilton chose whisky. The ambassador took nothing. He handed them the drinks and said, 'On a personal level, I consider I should have been told what was going on.'

'Until we had proof, everyone was suspect.'

Momentarily Billington's face clouded. 'How long had Walsingham been a spy?'

'According to what we've already discovered in London from the flat of the man Muffin, a long time. We might learn more when the banks open here tomorrow. Walsingham had what appears to be a safe deposit key on him: his wife insists she knows nothing about it.'

'What about her?'

'She's still to be questioned,' said Wilson. 'It's likely she was the link, from her past association.'

'I would have staked my reputation that Walsingham was sound,' said Billington. 'Not brilliant, but sound.'

'That's the sort of impression spies are trained to convey.'

'And the other fellow,' said Billington. 'What sort of man commits five murders?'

'A desperate one,' Wilson replied.

'Not any more,' said Naire-Hamilton. 'He's finished.' The Permanent Under Secretary looked directly at Wilson. 'And I mean that,' he said.

The empty place at the Politiburo table stood out like a child's gap-toothed smile. General Kalenin studiously ignored it, concentrating fixedly upon the First Secretary.

'An overwhelming success, Comrade General.'

It was fitting to be modest. 'It will be several days,' said Kalenin, 'before we can be completely sure.'

Zemskov frowned at the reservation. 'How long?' he said, wanting specifics.

'Two or three days.'

'We'll look forward to the meeting.'

And so would he, thought Kalenin; he'd wear his medals for the ceremony.

The butler, in dressing gown and pyjamas, tried to prevent their entry but the security men were accustomed to delaying tactics, bustling him aside the moment the door was opened into the Eaton Square apartment. Two took the stairs while another two waited for the lift. The fifth man insisted the butler take him through the servants' quarters and up the back stairs.

Rupert Willoughby awoke startled to find his bedroom full of men. 'What the ... ?'

'Rupert Willoughby?'

'Yes.'

'We've a warrant for your arrest, under the Treason Act,' said one of them.

'Treason?'

'We'd like you to get dressed and come with us.'

'I want to ring my solicitors.'

A security man moved the telephone away from the underwriter. The one holding the warrant said, 'Later. Just come with us now.'

26

They hadn't allowed him any water to wash or shave. Charlie had peed in the bucket and knew that the smell of the room clung to him. Jackson beckoned him from the doorway. Charlie got up slowly from the bed, stretching the cramp from his back. He'd spent the night hunched against the wall, knees beneath his chin, and felt lightheaded from sleeplessness. Charlie clutched at his unsupported clothing and shuffled out into the interrogation room. The arrangements were the same as before, except that there was a second man, in horn-rimmed glasses, at the recording table. He was seated behind a box file. But there was no chair for Charlie this time. Bastards, he thought. He stood with his legs apart, trying to keep his trousers up that way; they bagged at the waist.

'We'll discuss your defection,' said Wilson, as if there had only been a few minutes' interruption.

'There was no defection,' said Charlie.

'At the end of 1977 you went to the Soviet Union,'

'I did not.'

Wilson put out his hand and from the box file the bespectacled man produced a small wallet. Wilson leaned forward across the table and said, 'Is that your photograph?'

'Yes,' said Charlie curiously.

Wilson turned towards the recording equipment. 'Exhibit 1 that Charles Muffin has identified containing his photograph is an identity document, according him the rank of major in the KGB and establishing entry into the Soviet Union in November 1977.'

'This is nonsense.'

'We found everything in your flat,' said the director. 'And Walsingham's on-demand safe deposit box here in Rome. If he hadn't panicked, you'd have got away with it. He would have been dead, but you'd still have been free.'

Wilson was handed something else from the document box and held it up for Charlie. 'Is that your photograph attached to this card?'

'Of course it is.' Careful, he thought: he'd let the irritation show.

Again Wilson turned to the side table. 'Let the record show that Muffin has just acknowledged his photograph on the official authorization to concessions in certain restricted Moscow stores. It will be exhibit 2.'

'Why are you doing this?' demanded Charlie. 'You know it's not true.'

Wilson ignored the protest. 'Do you know what these are?' He held up some sort of decoration in his hand. With it was a long, official-looking form. Charlie saw the writing was cyrillic.

'I've never seen either before in my life,' said Charlie. He tried to reject the panic sweeping through him.

Once more Wilson spoke to his right. 'Exhibit 3 is the official decoration of the Hero of the Soviet Union, with a citation commending Charles Muffin for outstanding work on behalf of the security service of the Soviet Union.'

'It's not true!' said Charlie desperately. 'It's complete invention.'

Naire-Hamilton cupped his hand to Wilson. The director listened, and then said to Charlie, 'There's no point in extending this, is there? Why not admit it?'

'My name is Charlie Muffin,' he recited, in a name, rank and serial number monotone. 'In 1977 I disclosed to the Soviet Union the whereabouts in Vienna of the British and American intelligence directors, for personal reasons. That is all I have ever done. At no time beyond that have I had any contact with Russia.... ' He stared straight at Naire-Hamilton. 'I have killed no one.'

'What's that?' demanded Wilson.

'A Canadian passport,' said Charlie.

'Take it.'

Charlie held onto his trousers with his left hand and felt out with his right.

'What's the entry stamp, on page thirty-six?'

Charlie turned the pages awkwardly, supporting the document against his chest. 'Delhi,' he said.

'Did you, on 14 April, two days after the admission into India recorded on that date stamp, kill a British intelligence agent named Walter Thomison?'

'No!'

'What's the entry on page twenty-eight?'

Charlie fumbled through. 'Ankara.'

'Did you, on 27 August, one day after your arrival in Turkey, assassinate Rupert Bullock, a British intelligence agent attached to the embassy there?'

'This is a farce.... '

'Page forty-four,' stipulated Wilson.

Dully Charlie turned the pages. 'Bangkok.'

'Did you, on 3 October, four days after your arrival, shoot Peter Weighill, who had been identified to you as an intelligence operative working out of the British embassy in Thailand?'

'No,' said Charlie. His mind was misted by the accusations being made against him.

'Do you recognize these?' demanded the director, offering a fan spread of paper.

Charlie sighed. 'No,' he said.

Wilson went to the note table. 'This will be itemized as exhibit 5, the passport being exhibit 4,' he said. 'It consists of congratulatory cables, two signed personally by General Kalenin, commending Charlie Muffin on the success of his assassination of British agents attached to embassies in the three countries in which the Canadian passport numbered 18756 shows he had access.'

He'd let them play themselves out. There was nothing else he could do.

'Let the deposition show we are discussing what I shall identify as exhibit 6,' said Wilson. He offered it to Charlie. It was long, running to two pages and on flimsy paper that

Charlie remembered from intelligence briefings. 'Do you know this?'

'No.'

Wilson sat back, holding it loosely before him. 'It's your instruction sheet.'

'What instruction sheet?'

'Telling you what to do here,' said Wilson. 'Telling you that Henry Walsingham, a spy like you, had panicked after the caution from Moscow that he was under suspicion and intended organizing a robbery on the ambassador's safe, believing information incriminating him was being held there.... ' Wilson broke off. 'You were brilliant, getting to that safe as you did to find it wasn't so. Didn't Walsingham believe you when you told him there was nothing there?'

'Walsingham wasn't a spy.'

Wilson waved the paper. 'The instructions make it clear you were to kill him, because he'd become unstable. You had to improvise when the robbery went ahead, didn't you?'

'Like everything else alleged today, this is complete nonsense,' said Charlie. He spoke towards the recorder: if they were going to get the bullshit on tape, his denials were going to be there too.

'You knew Walsingham, didn't you: you were his control?'

'No.'

'We've proof,' said Wilson. 'We found the key, to the safe deposit box. It's all there.'

'I met Henry Walsingham the day after the robbery, at the ambassador's villa at Ostia. I had never met him before.'

Wilson reached for the document.

'Exhibit 7 will be listed as the Soviet message indicating initial control contact with Charlie Muffin,' he said. 'It contains a notation in Walsingham's handwriting confirming that the meeting took place on 10 June last year in Washington.'

Relief surged through Charlie. 'What was that date?'

'10 June!'

'No!' said Charlie triumphantly. 'And now it's in the record there's nothing you can do about it.'

As Charlie thought of Willoughby there was a kaleidoscope of imagery, of his meeting in the underwriter's office and then, intrusively, of a grey-suited man reading a magazine in the waiting room; the same grey-suited man who fell into step behind Clarissa as she walked past the Trevi fountain.

'Bastard!' said Charlie. But why? Hadn't he been the bigger bastard for what he'd done with Clarissa, willing though she might have been? Ironically it made things easier. He looked at the director. 'Rupert Willoughby can prove I wasn't in Washington on 10 June last year.' Charlie hesitated, arrested by another image – the crying, tear-stained face of Edith during one of their last rows. And her accusation, *'Nothing matters to you but survival does it Charlie ... nothing at all....'* She'd been right, as always. To Wilson he said, 'And it can be corroborated.'

It was a vast high-ceilinged room, already prepared for some of the conferences to be held during the forthcoming Summit. It was dominated by two tables arranged in a T; ministers sat at the top cross section and their advisers were spread away from them. Wires ribboned the floor, for the microphones set before each place and for the translations to be fed into the headsets clipped discreetly against each chair arm. Beyond the main seating arrangement was a small table, for the conference secretariat, and it was here that Billington, Wilson and Naire-Hamilton sat.

'I would like to say at the outset on behalf of my government that we greatly appreciate your understanding in allowing this discussion.' Naire-Hamilton fell easily into standard diplomatic verbosity. The London instructions were that he should lead the meeting, to spare Billington full responsibility as the permanent British representative.

'And, on behalf of *my* government, I want to make it clear that we consider what has taken place to be a flagrant breach of every diplomatic understanding,' said Guiseppe Belli. The Foreign Ministry official was a saturnine, sallow-complexioned man whose lightweight pinstripe matched Naire-Hamilton's in elegance. He made a striking contrast with Inspector Moro, who sat to his left. The third Italian,

Roberto Delcasta, was the deputy director of Italian intelligence, a slight, bespectacled man.

'There was no intention for it to be,' said Naire-Hamilton.

'How else can it be construed?' demanded Belli impatiently. His English was clipped and precise.

'As a sincere attempt on behalf of my country to avoid a scandal,' said Naire-Hamilton.

'How?' demanded Delcasta. 'The robbery had already created security doubts with other countries.'

Naire-Hamilton nodded for Wilson to take over. Succinctly, with no deviation from the rehearsed story, the intelligence director talked of the suspicion of a traitor within the British embassy, their efforts to locate him and the discovery of a man who had disgraced the service seven years earlier. As he spoke he stared intently at the three Italians facing him, aware of the slight relaxation of their attitude. It was fifteen minutes before he stopped, and at once Naire-Hamilton said, 'Throughout it has been the intention of the British government to limit the possibility of embarrassment for the Common Market Summit in a fortnight's time.'

'Cooperation would have achieved the same result,' said Belli.

Naire-Hamilton could not be deflected so easily. 'Until eight o'clock last night we saw it as an internal matter to be controlled within the privileged precincts of our own embassy. We had less than two hours to act when it turned out otherwise.'

'That is still no explanation for removing the body of the dead British national,' said Moro. 'Or seizing the man responsible. That is positive interference in an investigation being carried out by the Italian authorities.'

'I've already explained the purpose; the instinctive reaction was that to call the police risked the matter becoming public.' Naire-Hamilton was adamant.

'There has to be a satisfactory solution,' said Belli.

'Which is why we sought this meeting,' said Naire-Hamilton.

'What?' said the Italian.

'You had a robbery of a British ambassador, which was

distressing so close to the Summit,' said Wilson, realizing the offer would have to come from them. 'And from the palm print and blood samples you know you have discovered the thief.'

'So?' demanded Moro.

'It can't be too hard to invent an account of a successful police investigation, culminating in an attempted seizure during which the man was killed.'

'A story like that could never be contained within the civil police,' protested Delcasta.

'No need even to try,' said Wilson. 'Already it is known that Inspector Moro is attached to diplomatic protection. An attempted arrest by a security squad would be publicly acceptable. And also ensure secrecy.'

'It would also reassure other governments of the effectiveness of your diplomatic safeguard,' added Naire-Hamilton. 'And be a strong argument against increasing their own bodyguard contingent.'

'And you would look after your own problems?' said Belli.

'Absolutely,' said Naire-Hamilton.

'Which leaves the Summit,' said Belli.

'Which I'm also prepared to discuss,' said Naire-Hamilton.

Wilson looked curiously along his side of the table and then realized that the discussion had moved beyond the seizure on the Via Salaria.

'My government does not see it as an easy meeting,' said Belli.

'There are certain contentious issues,' said Naire-Hamilton.

'A possible dispute between us, I believe. About subsidy contributions.'

'I'm aware of the agenda,' said Naire-Hamilton.

'It is an item which my government would prefer not to have been included,' said Belli.

'I understand that the items for discussion are still subject to final agreement between the secretariat,' said Naire-Hamilton.

'That's also my understanding,' said Belli.

'I'm authorized to say that my government would greatly appreciate your discretion about the difficulties with our embassy.'

'And I'm authorized to bring it to a conclusion,' disclosed Belli.

'It would be unfortunate for there to be disagreements between our two governments.'

'I am sure it can be avoided.'

'Have I your guarantee on that?'

Again there was a pause before Naire-Hamilton replied. 'Yes,' he said. 'An absolute guarantee.'

Belli pushed back his chair, allowing a smile. Neither Delcasta nor Moro joined in. Wilson felt the meeting moving in their favour. He felt a rare admiration for the way Naire-Hamilton had conducted the negotiations.

'Any official investigation into what happened at the Via Salaria *could* provoke unwelcome publicity,' said Belli. He looked to Moro. 'Can we make it work?'

'With the greatest difficulty,' said Moro reluctantly. The anger was moving through the policeman, so that he found it hard to remain still.

'But it is *possible*?' pressed Belli.

'I suppose so.'

Belli returned to Naire-Hamilton. 'My government would also want an assurance that never again would you consider acting in such a fashion in our country.'

'Which I have given you, unhesitatingly,' said Naire-Hamilton at once.

Belli forced his public smile. 'I think we have an agreement.'

They shook hands. 'There has been no official transcript,' said Belli. 'It is important that we trust each other for the agreements to be kept.'

Wilson saw Moro look towards the extensive electronic equipment on the larger table and decided his earlier doubts were well founded.

'There will be no misunderstanding,' assured Naire-Hamilton.

*

They had used Billington's official car, with the glassed partition between them and the driver: Naire-Hamilton and Billington sat in the back with Wilson opposite on the jump seat.

'The PM won't like the concessions,' predicted Naire-Hamilton.

'There was no choice,' said Billington. 'The Italians had all the cards.'

'He'd set his mind on getting the subsidies properly distributed: it'll look a ridiculous climb-down.'

'Lesser of two evils,' said Billington.

Naire-Hamilton looked up at the intelligence director. 'Now that's resolved, we can go ahead as planned,' he said.

Wilson moved on the cramped seat. 'I want to question him further,' he said. 'That date is an odd disparity.'

Naire-Hamilton let the pause become obvious between them. 'We've pulled back from a potential disaster,' he said slowly.

'I want to avoid another one,' said Wilson.

27

They had allowed him coffee and bread for breakfast. Charlie guessed it must be mid-morning when they let him empty his bucket, but without any daylight it was difficult to judge. He shuffled across the basement, one hand at his trousers, the other through the wire grip of the pail, with Jackson leading and two men behind. It was a small toilet, obviously rarely used, but there was a hand basin. They made him keep the lavatory door open. Afterwards, without asking, Charlie went to the bowl, sluicing water into his face; there wasn't any soap, and when he looked around he realized there was no towel either.

'I don't suppose you'd let me have a razor?'

'Don't be bloody stupid,' said Jackson.

They formed up as before and marched back to the cell. The table and the recording equipment were still in place. The hope came quickly: they were checking what he'd said. The brief excursion made him aware of how cramped he was so he didn't squat again on the cot but kept pacing the small room. He thought back to the meeting with Willoughby in the office and then at dinner and then the visits to Ostia, willing himself to recall the conversations. There'd been unease, he remembered: and stupidly he'd dismissed it. But unease about what? A car that might have been following? No, more than that. A feeling that somebody had said or done something which was inconsistent. But what, among so much? It was like trying to climb out of a sandhole, constantly pulling the sides back in upon himself.

Charlie had to bunch his toes to prevent his scuffed old suedes sliding off and soon his feet began to ache, so he went back to the cot. The room beyond was completely silent. Once he stood, putting his ear to the door and then, without purpose, pushed at it. The door moved, slightly, against the bolts. He did it again more forcefully and waited. There was no reaction from outside.

Charlie jerked away, when the door suddenly opened. There was a man with a tray, and behind him was Henry Jackson. *'I'd like to kick the shit out of you.'* He'd get the chance, Charlie knew.

There was cold sausage, bread and more coffee. Because there was a knife and fork on the tray, the door was left open and Jackson remained inside. Charlie picked at the food, the nausea thick at the back of his throat.

'Missing the caviar and vodka?'

'Never touch the stuff.'

'You won't again.'

Charlie removed a piece of gristle from his mouth and examined it before sticking it on the side of his plate. He splayed his knife and fork and took up the coffee cup. 'Been in the department long?'

'Five years.'

'What's Wilson like?'

'The best damned director there is.'

'Reminds me of someone I once knew,' said Charlie.

'He got you,' said Jackson. 'And we knew all about Walsingham.'

Carefully Charlie replaced the coffee cup and took up the knife and fork. 'How?'

'The trap, of course. And we found out about the Communist party links in Australia.'

Charlie broke the stale bread into pieces. What did he have? A leak, which they believed they'd found. With a trap. And some Communist affiliation. And Walsingham, whom he knew *wasn't* the man. Plus his own curious involvement. It was like trying to make up a four-thousand-piece jigsaw that included a lot of sky and with no cover picture for a guide.

'Why wasn't Walsingham arrested?'

'We weren't ready,' said Jackson uncomfortably.

'And then you buggered it up,' said Charlie.

193

Jackson shook his head. 'You're the important one. And you know what I'd like to do?'

'Yes,' said Charlie. 'You already told me.'

Willoughby's habitual stoop was more marked and the suit looked creased and over-worn. His hand strayed in the familiar sweeping gesture towards his hair.

'What the hell's going on?' he said.

Wilson gestured for the tape to be activated and said, 'You are Rupert Willoughby?'

'Who are you?'

'Sir Alistair Wilson, the director of intelligence. My colleague here is with the government.'

Willoughby glanced at Charlie. 'What's he supposed to have done?'

'Do you know him?' asked Wilson.

'Of course I do.'

'Were you aware he was an agent of the Soviet Union?'

For a long time Willoughby didn't speak. At last he said, 'That's ridiculous: he worked for my father.'

'We're aware of his history,' said Wilson heavily. 'All of it.'

'I want a lawyer,' said Willoughby. 'My home was forcibly entered. I've been brought here without explanation. I'm saying no more until I'm allowed access to a lawyer.'

'You'll get one when we decide,' said Wilson.

'I want someone in higher authority.'

'We're the only authority here,' said Naire-Hamilton.

Charlie looked sadly at the underwriter: Willoughby was bent as if he were supporting a weight too heavy for him. Then he remembered the man in the grey suit. Charlie didn't feel any rancour. Willoughby had been more than justified in putting an inquiry agent onto him.

'At no time did Rupert Willoughby know what I had done,' Charlie interrupted. 'He knew I'd left the department, but not what the circumstances were. He's not guilty of any offence.'

'That's for us to decide,' said Naire-Hamilton.

'He thought my training might help with something his firm was finding difficult, that's all,' insisted Charlie.

Impatiently Wilson turned from Charlie back to Willoughby and said, 'Did you have any contact with this man in the summer of last year?'

'I do not know anything about the sort of activities you're suggesting,' said Willoughby.

'Did you have any contact in the summer of last year?' persisted Wilson.

'Yes.'

'When?'

'Around June, I suppose.'

'We're not interested in what you suppose,' said Wilson. 'When?'

'June,' said the underwriter.

'What date in June?'

'There was an exhibition of stamps, first in New York and then in Florida,' said Willoughby distantly. 'We covered them and I wanted some reassurance of protection. It would have been early in the month.'

'How early?' said Wilson.

'5 or 6 June,' said Willoughby. 'No,' he corrected, in sudden recollection. 'I'm sure it was the 7th. Definitely 7 June.'

'What precisely was 7 June?'

'The exhibition in New York.'

'And he was there?'

'Yes.'

'When did he return?'

'It ended on 9 July. He came back to London the following day.'

'Where were you?'

'Me? I don't understand.'

'New York or London?'

'London, of course.'

'So you don't know *where* he was in America?'

'New York, I've told you. And then Palm Beach.'

'What proof is there?'

'We spoke by telephone.'

'Every day?'

'Of course not every day: there wasn't the need. There must be hotel records.'

'Hotel records are of registration, not occupation,' said Wilson. 'You don't know whether he went down to Washington?'

'What would he do that for?'

'Answer the question.'

'I've no idea.'

'Did you speak to him by telephone on 10 June?'

'I can't remember as specifically as that.'

'Don't you keep a telephone log?'

'No.'

'This is pointless,' broke in Naire-Hamilton, 'as I always knew it would be. All we've got is confirmation of the meeting, which we hardly needed anyway.'

When the moment came Charlie held back, reluctant to speak. Not a murderer, he thought. Or a Soviet agent. And, from the conversation with Jackson, he knew there was one and that he was still undetected.

'I gave you another name,' he said to Wilson.

Clarissa Willoughby must have been brought direct from the yacht. She was wearing jeans, espadrilles and a sweater, and came through the door with an uncertain smile on her face, as if she suspected herself the victim of some elaborate practical joke. And then she saw her husband and Charlie, awkwardly holding up his trousers.

She looked to the intelligence director, who was obviously in charge, and said, 'What's going on? Who are you?'

'British security,' said Wilson, irritated at the constant need for identification.

The half-smile came again. 'This is a joke, isn't it?' Clarissa said.

'Do you know this man?' Wilson pointed to Charlie.

'Of course,' she snorted. Willoughby intercepted her look towards Charlie and the pain showed immediately.

'How?'

'What do you mean, how?'

196

'How did you meet him?'

'He was employed by my husband.'

'Was there an occasion when you were together in New York?'

Clarissa's eyes flickered back to Charlie again before she replied. 'Yes.'

Willoughby was intent upon his wife, oblivious to everything else in the room.

'When?'

'Is this important?'

'Yes.'

'Why?'

'He's a Soviet spy,' said Wilson bluntly. 'He's also a murderer.'

'Don't be so utterly absurd.'

'We have proof,' said Wilson. 'When did you arrive in New York last year?'

'8 June.'

'When did you encounter Charles Muffin?'

'The same day. We stayed at the same hotel.'

'What about the day after that?'

'There was a reception for the exhibition,' said Clarissa. 'We were all there.'

'Could he have left the reception? Gone to Washington for instance?'

'No,' said Clarissa. 'After the reception we had dinner. About eight of us.'

'And the following day, the 10th,' said Wilson. 'Could he have flown to Washington that day?'

'We were together throughout 10 June,' said Clarissa, looking back to Charlie. 'I remember it very well.'

'Where exactly?'

'Mostly in bed,' she said. 'We were together the entire day. And night.'

Jane Williams came back from the table in front of the chaise longue, where she had freshened Lady Billington's gin, and side by side they looked down at the jewellery boxes which were stacked in a neat wall, like building blocks in a nursery.

'I never thought you'd get them back so quickly. Or intact,' said the secretary.

'No,' said Lady Billington.

'Did you?'

The ambassador's wife shrugged. 'Didn't really think about it.'

Jane looked at her curiously. 'Weren't you *really* worried?' she said. 'I mean, to have lost all that.... '

'No,' said Lady Billington. 'I really wasn't; I wish I had been. It makes me feel a freak,' she sipped her drink. 'Do you know the only feeling I have?'

'What?'

'Sadness that for some reason I don't understand someone had to die over them.'

'Isn't it difficult to feel sad, after what Walsingham did?'

'Perhaps,' said Lady Billington. 'But he was a human being, whatever he'd done.'

They were still breathless after the lovemaking and Jane Williams lay with her head against Semingford's chest. He was moving his hand gently up and down her back and she realized, pleased, that he would want to make love again soon.

'I've had a reply from London,' said Semingford. 'About the pension. If I cashed it in, I'd have three thousand pounds after settling the overdraft.'

'Which isn't good enough for anything much, is it?' she said.

'No.'

'So what are you going to do?'

'I don't know.'

'Lady Billington says she feels like a freak, not being concerned about the jewellery.'

'She sounds it.'

'And that she feels sorry for Walsingham.'

She felt him pull away from her. 'What?'

'I know: that's what she said.'

'Was she drunk?'

'No more than usual.'

'They're moving heaven and earth to keep it quiet,' said Semingford. 'The Italians have agreed to cooperate.'

'It's difficult to imagine Walsingham doing it, isn't it?'

'It's funny,' said Semingford. 'Two days ago, before any of us knew, it was Henry. Now everyone's calling him Walsingham.'

'Wonder what it's like to be a spy?'

'How the hell would I know?' said Semingford, moving his hand between her legs.

28

In Rome, as in other embassies Sir Alistair Wilson had used, the communications centre was a room within a room, an inner shell fastened to the outer wall by a series of tubular struts from above and below, as well as from the sides. The inner compartment had been created by security workmen, guaranteeing that no monitoring device could have been built in. Access was across a drawbridge-type walkway which pulled up once the room was occupied. Cipher machines, like experimental typewriters, were banked against the left wall. At the back, a huge radio dominated the room, a pilot's cockpit of twitching dials and level measures. To the right were the security-cleared telex machines. The telephones were on a narrow bench to the left. There were three, all designated different colours. The white fed directly into Downing Street, equipped both here and at the other end with matching voice modulators which scrambled the conversation into unintelligible static unless it was cleared through a corrective device. This programme was changed weekly.

To remove the need for a cipher clerk, Naire-Hamilton had chosen the telephone. Before making the connection, he and Wilson had written out a full account and then attached notations to a master sheet, to ensure that the Permanent Under Secretary omitted nothing. He made the report with only occasional interruptions from London and by the time he'd finished his voice was hoarse and strained. There was a sheen of perspiration on his face when he finally replaced the telephone.

'He isn't happy,' he said.

'What the hell does he want?'

'He thinks the Italians got too much: that we allowed ourselves to be pressured.'

'Nonsense.'

'But easily said from the comfort of Downing Street.'

'What are the instructions?'

Naire-Hamilton hesitated. 'To terminate everything,' he said. 'He wants us out by tomorrow.'

'I think we should continue the debriefing.'

'To what purpose, for God's sake!'

'Why did Walsingham have the wrong date?'

'A simple enough mistake.'

'Men who keep records, like Walsingham and Muffin, don't make simple mistakes.'

'I'm fed up to the back teeth with sitting in that dungeon staring at that fellow holding up his trousers like some damned scarecrow,' said Naire-Hamilton.

'One more session,' said Wilson urgently

Jackson handed Charlie his belt as he entered the room. Seeing the start of apprehension, the supervisor smiled and said, 'Not yet. They're pissed off seeing you standing there as if you've shit yourself.'

Still without laces, Charlie had to shuffle once more into the interrogation room. The arrangement was as before, with no chair for him to sit on. Without the necessity of supporting his trousers, Charlie stood with feet apart with his hands clasped loosely behind his back. It was the sort of insolent at-ease that had driven the parade sergeants mad. Wilson didn't like it either.

'How long had you been the liaison between Moscow and Walsingham?' said the director.

'I was never the liaison. Until the day at the villa, I'd never set eyes on him.'

Wilson was handed something from the folder. 'This will be exhibit 10,' he said towards the recording machine. He offered it to Charlie. 'Who is this?'

'Who do you think?' said Charlie. It must have been taken by a hidden camera: it looked like a London street but he couldn't be sure.

'I want the deposition to show that this photograph of Charles Muffin was recovered from the safe deposit box in the name of Henry Walsingham. Attached to it were instructions, upon identification, for the contact meeting in Washington. Those instructions were dated February of last year.'

Something pricked at Charlie's memory and he groped for it, like a man trying to distinguish a half-formed shape in a fog.

'Quite obviously it was planted there,' said Charlie.

'Walsingham knew you.'

'He didn't know me until we met at the villa.'

'There'd been a previous time, in Washington.'

'Bullshit.'

'You'd been identified to him, for the Washington meeting.'

'The meeting!' Charlie shouted the words. 'That's where it went wrong.'

'What *are* you talking about?' said Wilson.

Charlie didn't respond at once. Then the answers came like a flood that follows the initial trickle through the dam wall. It had taken him a bloody long time; it wouldn't have done once.

'Four days ago I made contact with the man who robbed Billington's safe,' said Charlie. 'The man I found dead at the apartment.'

'Emilio Fantani,' said Wilson.

'I never knew his name. I recognized him then from the hand injury the police talked about. It was in Harry's Bar on the Via Veneto. The staff there can confirm it. It'll be independent corroboration.'

'Of what?'

'That a meeting took place.'

'It had to,' said Wilson. 'Your instructions were to silence Walsingham. And Fantani was the link.'

'What was the only thing that would have mattered to Fantani?'

Wilson considered the question. 'The pay-off, I suppose.

That's what he'd been promised by Walsingham, according to the message from Moscow.'

'The pay-off,' agreed Charlie. 'The pay-off figure was wrong.'

'What do you mean?'

'You believe Walsingham staged the robbery on his own initiative?'

Wilson was beginning to feel slightly uneasy.

'The insurance was for one and a half million pounds,' said Charlie. 'Fantani demanded a ransom of twenty-five per cent.'

'Well?'

'What's twenty-five per cent of one and a half million?'

'Three hundred and seventy-five thousand,' said Wilson.

'But Fantani asked for five hundred thousand,' said Charlie. 'You've recovered the money. Count it yourself.'

'What's the significance?'

'Fantani knew the policy was a replacement one, with adjustments for the increased value of the jewellery that took its cost up to two million. And he couldn't have learned that from Walsingham, because Walsingham couldn't have known those details.'

'*You* did.'

'But I wasn't working with him, according to you!'

Wilson and Naire-Hamilton exchanged worried looks. In the pause the final piece of the puzzle fitted into place, 'The timing,' said Charlie, more to himself than his interrogators. 'Walsingham was at the Via Salaria earlier than I said.'

'What are you saying?' demanded Wilson.

'You're going to kill me, aren't you?'

Naire-Hamilton twitched nervously towards the turning tapes and then back to Charlie. He didn't speak. Neither did Wilson.

'I know who did it,' said Charlie. 'I know who your spy is.'

'Who?'

'A deal,' said Charlie. 'My life for the name of the spy. If not, you can go to hell.'

Willoughby and Clarissa were put aboard the same RAF

plane that had brought the underwriter to Rome and seated next to each other. It occurred to neither of them to object, which they could have done because Clarissa was not under any detention. The aircraft had been flying for almost an hour before Willoughby spoke.

'I know what happened in Rome.'

She glanced at him but said nothing.

'I trapped you,' he said with bitter triumph. 'I could have got anyone to do the security check but I knew he was desperate and so I tricked him into coming. I guessed what had happened in New York and I knew you'd come rutting after him instead of going to Menton. You were watched the whole time.'

'You needn't have wasted your money,' she said wearily. 'All you had to do was ask.'

'You're a whore,' he said.

'Haven't we had these recriminations before?'

'I'm divorcing you.'

'You've said that before too.'

'How could you!' said Willoughby. 'With him! Even before you knew the sort of man he is.'

Clarissa smiled wanly. 'Actually it wasn't easy,' she said. 'He didn't want to at first. Said it would be letting you down.'

'You mean you seduced him?'

'Yes,' she said. 'I suppose I did. It was a joke at first.'

'It means nothing to you, does it?'

'No,' she agreed. 'Not normally.'

He looked at her disbelievingly. 'Surely you don't think that you love him!'

'Yes,' she said. 'I think I do. Insane, isn't it?'

Wilson was seated in the small office that had been allocated to them in the embassy. Naire-Hamilton was still striding about the room, the more nervous of the two. His hands twitched about him.

'Do you realize the risk you're taking?'

'Do you realize what it is if I don't?'

'What authority have you got for giving in to his demand?'

'None,' admitted the intelligence director. 'If I hadn't given it he wouldn't have told us.'

'Bloody guttersnipe!'

'What if he's right?'

There was a knock at the door. 'Mrs Walsingham is here,' said Jackson.

At first Igor Solomatin remained stiffly to attention but Kalenin seated him and watched him gradually relax under the congratulations.

'You made no contact afterwards with the embassy?' asked Kalenin.

'I considered it safer not to.'

'Quite right.'

'There's little doubt that it worked, though,' said Solomatin hurriedly. 'There would have been news of an arrest if it hadn't.'

Seeing the man's anxiety, Kalenin said, 'It was a brilliant operation.'

'Thank you.' Solomatin was visibly relieved.

'There is a vacancy upon my staff of deputies,' said Kalenin. 'I'd like you to take it. You'd be responsible for initiating clandestine activities: precisely the sort of thing you've just done.'

'I'm honoured, Comrade General,' said Solomatin.

Kalenin knew his turn was coming. The Politburo meeting was only two days away.

29

Sir Hector Billington came hesitantly into the basement. A chair had been set on the side opposite the recording table and the Permanent Under Secretary showed him to it.

'We appreciate your coming,' said Naire-Hamilton.

'Are you *sure* this is necessary?'

'Essential,' said Wilson.

'How can I help you?' asked Billington.

'On some points he has raised,' said Naire-Hamilton, nodding towards Charlie.

Billington regarded Charlie with undisguised contempt. 'I'm to be questioned by *him*!'

'It won't take long.'

'I sincerely hope not.'

'Proceed,' Wilson said to Charlie.

'You telephoned me at the hotel to tell me where to meet Fantani?' Charlie couldn't afford to make one mistake.

Billington appeared embarrassed at the reminder of co-operation. 'Yes,' he said.

'Where was the meeting?'

'I think it was Harry's Bar.'

'At the villa the day after the robbery the police decided to limit the information publicly released. And the value was put at the original assessment, one and a half million pounds.'

Billington looked annoyed. 'What is the purpose of this?'

'Establishing guilt,' said the Permanent Under Secretary.

Billington returned to Charlie. 'Go on,' he said, stiffly.

'When I met Fantani, he demanded twenty-five per cent of the insurance value, and put it at five hundred thousand.

And that was the new, not the old, valuation.'

'I don't see your point,' said Billington.

'Let's try something else then,' said Charlie. 'When I talked to Fantani, he made a remark about there being no danger of his being arrested, because police had fingerprints, not palm prints. And that he had destroyed the jacket, so there would be no fibre tracings.'

Billington gave an exaggerated shrug.

'No information was publicly released about a palm print being found at the villa,' said Charlie. 'Or of cloth fibres. But I told you, after I'd talked to Inspector Moro.'

Billington's eyes pebbled in abrupt realization, colour flooding his face. He jerked around to Naire-Hamilton and Wilson and said, 'Of all the ... ! Are you allowing this man to cross-examine me, as if I'm involved in some way in a robbery of my own property!'

'You're a cautious man,' persisted Charlie. 'Everyone kept telling me that when I first went to the villa. And you obviously are. I've never seen so many alarms. So why didn't you put away the jewellery your wife had worn that night? That's what a properly cautious man would have done; unless he didn't want to risk premature discovery.'

'I want this stopped!' demanded Billington.

'And in the end it was premature,' said Charlie. 'Your wife told me what happened, because she was in the dressing room. About your saying, "Oh! My God!" *immediately* you opened the safe. But you couldn't have seen anything immediately you opened the safe, could you? All the jewellery was kept in cases, which had to be opened. Your wife mentioned that too. "When we opened the cases, everything was gone," she said.'

Billington was holding himself stiffly in the chair. He stared fixedly at Charlie. 'Finish,' he said. 'I want you to finish.'

'There's only one more thing,' said Charlie. 'On the day of the robbery I talked a lot of quasi-legal rubbish, making it up as I went along, to persuade you to agree to a settlement idea. And you didn't challenge me. But you're a *lawyer* with an Oxford degree. So you would have known I was talking nonsense.'

Billington rose to his feet, standing with his back to Charlie and looking down at Naire-Hamilton and Wilson. 'From the start,' he said, only just managing the evenness to his voice, 'your behaviour has been appalling. I have permitted it because of the circumstances that were explained to me, making every excuse and every allowance. But this I will not excuse. Today I am going to request the Foreign Secretary to recall me to London. There I shall demand a full inquiry. Even to have considered asking me to confront these demented ramblings of a known traitor, to imagine any need for me to explain myself, is scandalous.'

'Sit down,' said Wilson.

Jill Walsingham came like a sleepwalker into the room. Solicitously Wilson helped her into a chair and nodded towards Jackson. The supervisor appeared with a water glass and put it by her on the recording table. She was going through the deadening period of shock, when the senses retreat.

'This won't take long,' assured Wilson.

'I want to know what's going on!' insisted Billington from the facing chair.

'You will,' said Wilson. 'I promise you will.' He looked back to the woman. 'You told me you were frightened, after I found out about the Communist association in Australia?'

Jill Walsingham kept her eyes fixed just above their heads, seeing and hearing nothing.

'Mrs Walsingham,' said Wilson sharply.

She shuddered, concentrating upon him. 'After I challenged you about Australia you were frightened?'

'Yes.'

'Why?'

'Because it was silly.'

'Why was it silly?'

'Because it didn't mean anything. We told you why it didn't mean anything, but you didn't believe us.'

'Tell me what you decided to do,' asked Wilson softly.

'To be careful,' she said at once.

'Why would you need to be careful?'

'Because you were trying to trap us.'

'I demand to know what's going on!' interrupted Billington. 'This is obscene.'

'Shut up,' said Wilson irritably.

'There'll be an account for this.'

Wilson ignored the ambassador. 'Were you careful?' he said.

She nodded, like a child anxious to please. 'Henry was very good, you know. He studied at the electronic surveillance establishment at Cheltenham.'

'How were you careful?' encouraged Wilson.

'Any contact,' she said. 'Particularly on the telephone.'

Wilson turned to the ambassador, who was sitting rigid in his chair.

'Tell me about the telephone calls on the night your husband died,' said the director.

'Henry wasn't back from the embassy. A man called for him and I told him to ring back.'

'Who was the man?'

'He said he was from the insurance company.'

'Did you know him?'

'No.'

Wilson nodded and the operator of the recording apparatus depressed a button. Into the room came the sound of Charlie Muffin's voice, during his questioning of the ambassador. ' ... On the day of the robbery, I talked a lot of quasi-legal rubbish, making it up as I went along.... ' Wilson flicked his hand and the man stopped the tape.

'Is that the voice?'

'It sounds like it.'

'Then what happened?'

'I told Henry when he got back from the embassy. He said it was important: that an arrangement was being set up to recover the jewellery and he would be involved. The second telephone call came after about ten minutes.'

'Who was it?'

'Henry said it was the insurance man: a name like Mutton or Mullen or something.'

'What was the point of the conversation?'

'A meeting,' said the woman. 'Henry had to go to the Via Salaria, where the jewellery was to be bought back.'

'Was there a time given?'

'Eight forty-five.'

'Then what happened?'

'We had plenty of time; it wasn't even seven. We decided to eat first.'

'Did you?'

She shook her head. 'There was another call, changing the time. Henry had to be there at eight.'

'Was it the insurance man again?'

She frowned at the question. 'No,' she said, turning into the room. She pointed to Billington, 'Him.'

'This is incredible!' erupted the ambassador. 'I'll have your jobs for this.'

'Did you answer the telephone?'

'No. Henry did.'

'So how do you know it was the ambassador?'

'He said so at once.'

'You're listening to the words of a spy's wife,' said Billington, his voice stretched. 'A known Communist.'

Wilson gave another instruction to the technician alongside. Charlie Muffin's disembodied voice filled the room.

'*Make it eight forty-five.*'

'*Where?*'

'*35 Via Salaria: centre door. I'll be waiting for you.*'

'*What about the ambassador?*'

'*Tell him.*'

'*What about the police?*'

'*I'll tell them when it's over: it could all be a hoax.*'

Jill Walsingham began to sob, her fat body trembling with emotion. She put a handkerchief to her face, mumbling through it. 'I'm sorry ... very sorry.... '

Walsingham's voice came over her apology. '*You don't really believe that, do you?*'

'*I'd be wasting everybody's bloody time if I didn't.*'

'*Good luck.*'

'*Yeah.*'

'I want to say something,' said Billington. 'I want.... '

'I told you to be quiet,' said Wilson.

There was a brief smear of static on the tape, then the sound of a telephone being dialled. Billington's voice came at once onto the line. The intonation of respect was obvious. *'The Via Salaria,'* said the security man's voice, *'Eight forty-five.'*

'Are you sure?'

'Not until it's happened.'

'I'll be here at the embassy.'

'I'll call you as soon as it's confirmed as genuine.'

The break appeared the same as before, but this time there was no dialling tone because the call was incoming.

'I'm glad I caught you.'

'Yes, ambassador?'

'The man who called me about the meeting in Harry's Bar ... he's been on again. He says the hand-over time has been changed to eight o'clock.'

'I can't contact the insurance man: I don't know where he is. All he said was something about Milan and an autostrada.'

'I'd like you to go there.'

'Yes,' said Walsingham's voice.

'Mrs Walsingham,' said Wilson. 'What did you do after I challenged you about the Communist party membership?'

She looked up from her handkerchief. 'Recorded all the telephone conversations, of course. I told you, Henry graduated at electronic eavesdropping. He was very good.' She started to cry again.

It was a celebration and so there had been champagne – French because of Berenkov's preference. Valentina was already slightly drunk, giggling too eagerly at things that weren't really funny. Kalenin and Berenkov were tipsy too, laughing with her.

Berenkov raised his glass, spilling some wine as he did so and going through an exaggerated performance of mopping it up with his napkin before continuing. 'A toast,' he declared. 'To General Valery Ivanovich Kalenin, a member of the Politburo of the Union of Soviet Socialist Republics.'

'Not yet,' said Kalenin.

'Not long to wait,' said Berenkov. 'Only until tomorrow.'

'Yes,' agreed Kalenin, suddenly sobered by the realization. 'Only until tomorrow.'

30

It was quiet in the basement after the removal of Charlie Muffin and Walsingham's wife. Billington sat in the concentrated pool of light, all the bombast and protest gone.

'How long?' demanded Wilson. The director was aware of how close they had come to making a mistake and the anger he felt towards himself was discernible in his voice.

Billington didn't respond immediately, remaining with his head lolled forward against his chest.

'I said, how long!'

The ambassador stirred and looked about him, like someone awakening from a deep sleep. He blinked at Wilson. 'So very long,' he said distantly.

'I want to know precisely.'

'Years,' said Billington. He made an effort, straightening in his chair. 'I didn't want to,' he said, his voice stronger. 'Not ideological ... nothing like that.'

'Why then?'

'Difficult now to remember what he even looked like, clearly. I've tried, really tried! Isn't that ridiculous?'

'Who?' prompted Wilson. He was controlled now, cajoling, knowing that it would come out at Billington's pace, with only the need to prompt occasionally..

'Didn't you ever have a special friend, when you were at school? Get drawn to a particular person?'

'No.' The story was sadly familiar.

'It wasn't serious ... I mean, I didn't continue it. Not like that at all: it's just something that happens. Part of growing up.'

Wilson made a note to check if the other man had

succumbed to similar pressure.

'How long after you left university?' said Naire-Hamilton.

'Several years,' said Billington. 'I was Third Secretary in Washington. I'd passed everything by then: knew it was all going to be wonderful. Everything was going to be wonderful. Engaged to Norah: the wedding was already planned ... royalty came, you know.... '

'What happened in Washington?' said Wilson.

'He was a polite man. Good English. At first I thought he was an American from the State Department. Approached me at a reception and began talking about Oxford. Said he'd been there. Rang me afterwards and suggested lunch, and so we met. And then he showed me a picture....' He looked up at the intelligence chief, his eyes flooded. 'I didn't know it had been taken. There'd been a Finals party, with a lot to drink. We were saying goodbye to each other; isn't that ironic! That was when it ended. The last time.'

'What did he say, this man in Washington?' said Naire-Hamilton.

'He talked of my career and the marriage. Said how quickly it would all be over, if there were any exposure. Didn't ask for much; he could have got it from a reference book, in the library, if he'd waited for the annual list. Just the details of the trade figures. Not even classified.'

'You gave them to him?'

Billington nodded. 'The next time it was for something a little more important, some papers on a warplane the Americans were thinking of buying from us. And then details of the aircraft itself, because it had just been shown at Farnborough and was new, some of the equipment still secret.'

'Didn't you protest?'

'Of course,' said Billington. 'And then they showed me more pictures. Not of Oxford this time. In Washington, with me meeting the man who'd first approached me, exchanging the first package. He'd gone back to Moscow by then. A known Russian agent, they said: how would that look, with the other photograph?'

'So you went on handing over things that were more and

more important?' said Wilson.

'But I had to, don't you see! If I hadn't I'd have been disgraced ... the family would have been disgraced. We've got one of the finest names in the diplomatic service!'

With a sense of rising disgust, Wilson wondered how long it had taken Billington to lobotomize himself against the guilt. 'What about the assassinations?' he said.

'I didn't want that,' said Billington urgently. 'I warned them of the danger....' He hesitated at the sudden stiffness in the director's face. Haltingly he added, 'I was told it was a policy decision: that I had to do it.'

'How many did you identify?' Wilson had to guard against the possibility that the Russians had suspended the killings, when they realized Rome had been uncovered, intending to resume them later.

'Three,' said Billington. 'New Delhi, Ankara and Bangkok.'

The recollections came abruptly, frigid pictures of calm-faced men with their chests torn apart. 'What about the robbery?' Wilson said.

'Had to do somuch,' said Billington petulantly. 'Not just the alarms and the combinations. Had to threaten withdrawal of the policy from Willoughby, unless the check was made. By then they'd discovered what the man Muffin did for him: claimed his involvement would create added confusion. They were very excited when it worked. Said the coincidence of his being in America at the same time as Walsingham made it perfect.'

'Who told them about Walsingham?'

'I didn't want to,' said Billington defensively. 'They knew about the business in Australia: insisted it was ideal when I found it wasn't on his record.'

'Haven't we heard enough?' said Naire-Hamilton, as disgusted as the director. 'Others can take over.'

Before Wilson could reply, the ambassador continued, 'You will help me, won't you? Now that you know I didn't have any choice. I'll resign, of course. But I don't want a scandal. There's the family to think of. Norah, too.'

'I know just how I'm going to treat you,' promised Wilson.

'It will be brilliant if it works,' said the Permanent Under Secretary.

'I'm going to make it work,' said Wilson vehemently. 'It isn't possible to recover the situation but I want to undo as much of the damage as I can.'

'I'm sorry I tried to hurry things,' said Naire-Hamilton. 'We got it right in the end, thank God.'

Naire-Hamilton laughed, the relief obvious. 'Such stupid mistakes, weren't they? Why the hell provide a positive date for America, for God's sake? If it hadn't been for that, we wouldn't have listened to anything else the damned man had to say.'

'It's always the small things,' said Wilson. He paused. 'And the ability to spot them.'

Reminded of Charlie Muffin, Naire-Hamilton looked toward the closed door of the box-room cell, with two men on guard outside. 'Brilliant idea if it works,' he said again.

Charlie was using the bucket when Wilson came into the room. He turned his back, hurriedly zipping his fly. 'Sorry,' he said and was then unsure what he'd apologized for.

'If it hadn't been for the disparity of the meeting time, he'd have got away with it,' said the director.

'It should have occurred to me before,' said Charlie. 'It would have, once.'

'We were lucky with the tape,' conceded the director. 'It wouldn't have meant much without it.'

Charlie realized it was automatic to remain standing respectfully in Wilson's presence. So much like Sir Archibald Willoughby, he thought. One reflection prompted another. What would happen to Rupert and Clarissa? It was inevitable, he supposed, but he still regretted being the cause of their collapse.

'Did Billington break?'

Wilson nodded. 'Full confession,' he said.

'There usually is,' said Charlie. 'It's the relief.' Now they'd got what they wanted from Billington, there was no reason why they should keep the undertaking. He had no way to make them: in their position he'd have made the same promise without any intention of keeping it.

'I'm going to turn him,' disclosed Wilson. 'I'm going to have him kept here as ambassador and I'm going to watch his every move and I'm going to feed Moscow everything I want.'

Charlie nodded approvingly. 'For that to work, they'll need to be convinced the disinformation was successful.'

'Of course,' agreed Wilson. 'They've no reason to doubt it.'

'It'll need something more,' insisted Charlie. 'Something public.'

'A scapegoat,' said Wilson at once. 'But I've got one, haven't I, Charlie?'

The occasion demanded medals should be worn, and, as he walked towards the assembled Politburo, Kalenin heard them clinking together. The reception was taking place in the larger, official room, with the enormous portraits of Lenin between the furled Soviet flags. Because it was the only ceremony of the day, the other twelve members were freshly pressed and formal, with none of the casualness of the encounters in the smaller committee room.

'It's time for congratulations,' announced the First Secretary when Kalenin came to a halt before him.

Kalenin bowed his head in a curt greeting but did not respond.

'The operation has been a complete and overwhelming success,' said Zemskov. 'On behalf of the Politburo, I formally thank you.'

'I did my duty,' said Kalenin. He wanted the record to show modesty.

'There has been discussion before your arrival,' said Zemskov, making the announcement properly formal. 'It delights me, Comrade General, to declare that, in accordance with the power vested in it between conferences of the Supreme Soviet, the Politburo has today unanimously elected you to serve with it, as a replacement for Comrade Kastanazy.'

The First Secretary thrust out his hand. Kalenin took it

and then bent forward for the obligatory kiss on either cheek. The formality eased. There was more handshaking and kissing and then attendants appeared with vodka and champagne.

Zemskov held his glass towards the KGB chief. 'There is someone else who should rightly be here with us, sharing this celebration,' he said.

'There has been a message from Rome,' said Kalenin. 'He's operating normally again.'

Epilogue

' ... Charles Edward Muffin, the charges against you are that being a servant of Her Majesty's government and a signatory to the Official Secrets Act, you did on divers dates.... '

Charlie stood with his hands lightly against the dock rail, only half concentrating upon the drone. He moved his toes in the luxury of expanded suede: they'd allowed him his own clothes for the hearing and for the first time in a week his feet were free from those bloody prison-issue boots.

' ... apply once more for a formal remand for seven days,' a man in a white wig and black gown was saying, ' ... at such time the Crown would hope to be in a position to propose a date for the full proceedings to begin.... '

It was an in-camera hearing, the number of people in court limited. Sir Alistair Wilson was directly behind the prosecuting counsel. There hadn't been any contact in prison, since the return from Italy, and Charlie expected some indication now, but the intelligence director didn't turn towards the dock. When the hell were they going to let him know? He'd survived, thought Charlie. But for what?

Bestselling Thriller/Suspense

☐ See You Later, Alligator	William F. Buckley	£2.50
☐ Hell is Always Today	Jack Higgins	£1.75
☐ Brought in Dead	Harry Patterson	£1.95
☐ Maxwell's Train	Christopher Hyde	£2.50
☐ Russian Spring	Dennis Jones	£2.50
☐ Nightbloom	Herbert Lieberman	£2.50
☐ Basikasingo	John Matthews	£2.95
☐ The Secret Lovers	Charles McCarry	£2.50
☐ Fletch	Gregory Mcdonald	£1.95
☐ Green Monday	Michael M. Thomas	£2.95
☐ Someone Else's Money	Michael M. Thomas	£2.50
☐ Black Ice	Colin Dunne	£2.50
☐ Blind Run	Brian Freemantle	£2.50
☐ The Proteus Operation	James P. Hogan	£3.50
☐ Miami One Way	Mike Winters	£2.50

Prices and other details are liable to change

ARROW BOOKS, BOOKSERVICE BY POST, PO BOX 29, DOUGLAS, ISLE OF MAN, BRITISH ISLES

NAME ....

ADDRESS ....

....

....

Please enclose a cheque or postal order made out to Arrow Books Ltd. for the amount due and allow the following for postage and packing.

U.K. CUSTOMERS: Please allow 22p per book to a maximum of £3.00.

B.F.P.O. & EIRE: Please allow 22p per book to a maximum of £3.00.

OVERSEAS CUSTOMERS: Please allow 22p per book.

Whilst every effort is made to keep prices low it is sometimes necessary to increase cover prices at short notice. Arrow Books reserve the right to show new retail prices on covers which may differ from those previously advertised in the text or elsewhere.

Bestselling Fiction

☐ Toll for the Brave	Jack Higgins	£2.25
☐ Basikasingo	John Matthews	£2.95
☐ Where No Man Cries	Emma Blair	£2.50
☐ Saudi	Laurie Devine	£2.95
☐ The Clogger's Child	Marie Joseph	£2.50
☐ The Gooding Girl	Pamela Oldfield	£2.95
☐ The Running Years	Claire Rayner	£2.75
☐ Duncton Wood	William Horwood	£3.50
☐ Aztec	Gary Jennings	£3.95
☐ Colours Aloft	Alexander Kent	£2.95
☐ The Volunteers	Douglas Reeman	£2.75
☐ The Second Lady	Irving Wallace	£2.95
☐ The Assassin	Evelyn Anthony	£2.50
☐ The Pride	Judith Saxton	£2.50
☐ The Lilac Bus	Maeve Binchy	£2.50
☐ Fire in Heaven	Malcolm Bosse	£3.50

Prices and other details are liable to change

ARROW BOOKS, BOOKSERVICE BY POST, PO BOX 29, DOUGLAS, ISLE OF MAN, BRITISH ISLES

NAME ....

ADDRESS ....

....

....

Please enclose a cheque or postal order made out to Arrow Books Ltd. for the amount due and allow the following for postage and packing.

U.K. CUSTOMERS: Please allow 22p per book to a maximum of £3.00.

B.F.P.O. & EIRE: Please allow 22p per book to a maximum of £3.00.

OVERSEAS CUSTOMERS: Please allow 22p per book.

Whilst every effort is made to keep prices low it is sometimes necessary to increase cover prices at short notice. Arrow Books reserve the right to show new retail prices on covers which may differ from those previously advertised in the text or elsewhere.

Bestselling Fiction

☐ Hiroshima Joe	Martin Booth	£2.95
☐ Voices on the Wind	Evelyn Anthony	£2.50
☐ The Pianoplayers	Anthony Burgess	£2.50
☐ Prizzi's Honour	Richard Condon	£2.95
☐ Queen's Play	Dorothy Dunnett	£3.50
☐ Duncton Wood	William Horwood	£3.50
☐ In Gallant Company	Alexander Kent	£2.50
☐ The Fast Men	Tom McNab	£2.95
☐ A Ship With No Name	Christopher Nicole	£2.95
☐ Contact	Carl Sagan	£3.50
☐ Uncle Mort's North Country	Peter Tinniswood	£2.50
☐ Fletch	Gregory Mcdonald	£1.95
☐ A Better World Than This	Marie Joseph	£2.95
☐ The Lilac Bus	Maeve Binchy	£2.50
☐ The Gooding Girl	Pamela Oldfield	£2.95

Prices and other details are liable to change

ARROW BOOKS, BOOKSERVICE BY POST, PO BOX 29, DOUGLAS, ISLE OF MAN, BRITISH ISLES

NAME ....

ADDRESS ....

....

....

Please enclose a cheque or postal order made out to Arrow Books Ltd. for the amount due and allow the following for postage and packing.

U.K. CUSTOMERS: Please allow 22p per book to a maximum of £3.00.

B.F.P.O. & EIRE: Please allow 22p per book to a maximum of £3.00.

OVERSEAS CUSTOMERS: Please allow 22p per book.

Whilst every effort is made to keep prices low it is sometimes necessary to increase cover prices at short notice. Arrow Books reserve the right to show new retail prices on covers which may differ from those previously advertised in the text or elsewhere.

A Selection of Arrow Bestsellers

☐ Live Flesh	Ruth Rendell	£2.75
☐ Contact ·	Carl Sagan	£3.50
☐ Yeager	Chuck Yeager	£3.95
☐ The Lilac Bus	Maeve Binchy	£2.50
☐ 500 Mile Walkies	Mark Wallington	£2.50
☐ Staying Off the Beaten Track	Elizabeth Gundrey	£4.95
☐ A Better World Than This	Marie Joseph	£2.95
☐ No Enemy But Time	Evelyn Anthony	£2.95
☐ Rates of Exchange	Malcolm Bradbury	£3.50
☐ For My Brother's Sins	Sheelagh Kelly	£3.50
☐ Carrott Roots	Jasper Carrott	£3.50
☐ Colours Aloft	Alexander Kent	£2.95
☐ Blind Run	Brian Freemantle	£2.50
☐ The Stationmaster's Daughter	Pamela Oldfield	£2.95
☐ Speaker for the Dead	Orson Scott Card	£2.95
☐ Football is a Funny Game	Ian St John and Jimmy Greaves	£3.95
☐ Crowned in a Far Country	Princess Michael of Kent	£4.95

Prices and other details are liable to change

ARROW BOOKS, BOOKSERVICE BY POST, PO BOX 29, DOUGLAS, ISLE OF MAN, BRITISH ISLES

NAME ....

ADDRESS ....

....

....

Please enclose a cheque or postal order made out to Arrow Books Ltd. for the amount due and allow the following for postage and packing.

U.K. CUSTOMERS: Please allow 22p per book to a maximum of £3.00.

B.F.P.O. & EIRE: Please allow 22p per book to a maximum of £3.00.

OVERSEAS CUSTOMERS: Please allow 22p per book.

Whilst every effort is made to keep prices low it is sometimes necessary to increase cover prices at short notice. Arrow Books reserve the right to show new retail prices on covers which may differ from those previously advertised in the text or elsewhere.